YOUNG
STAR
TRAVELERS

*Anthologies edited by Isaac Asimov, Martin H.
Greenberg, and Charles G. Waugh:*

YOUNG MUTANTS
YOUNG EXTRATERRESTRIALS
YOUNG MONSTERS
YOUNG GHOSTS

YOUNG STAR TRAVELERS

EDITED BY

Isaac Asimov,
Martin H. Greenberg,
and Charles G. Waugh

HARPER & ROW, PUBLISHERS

Library of Congress Cataloging-in-Publication Data
Main entry under title:
Young star travelers.

Summary: A collection of nine science fiction
stories about children who have traveled in space.
1. Science fiction, American. 2. Science fiction,
English. [1. Space flight—Fiction. 2. Science fiction.
3. Short stories] I. Asimov, Isaac, 1920–
II. Greenberg, Martin Harry. III. Waugh, Charles.
PZ5.Y8517 1986   [Fic]   85-45276
ISBN 0-06-020178-9
ISBN 0-06-020179-7 (lib. bdg.)

Acknowledgments

"If I Forget Thee, Oh Earth . . ." by Arthur C. Clarke. Copyright © 1951; renewed © 1979 by Arthur C. Clarke. Reprinted by permission of the Scott Meredith Literary Agency, Inc., 845 Third Ave., New York, NY 10022.

"Berserker's Prey" by Fred Saberhagen. Copyright © 1967 by Galaxy Publishing Corporation. Reprinted by permission of the author.

"Call Me Proteus" by Edward Wellen. Copyright © 1973 by UPD Publishing Corporation. Reprinted by permission of the author.

"Teddi" by Andre Norton. Copyright © 1973 by Western Publishing Company. Reprinted by permission of the Larry Sternig Literary Agency.

"The Gambling Hell and the Sinful Girl" by Katherine MacLean. Copyright © 1974 by the Condé Nast Publications, Inc., reprinted by permission of the author and the author's agent, Virginia Kidd.

"Invasion Report" by Theodore R. Cogswell. Copyright © 1954 by Galaxy Publishing Corporation; copyright renewed © 1982 by Theodore R. Cogswell. Reprinted by permission of the author.

"A Start in Life" by Arthur Sellings. Copyright © 1954 by Galaxy Publishing Corporation. Reprinted by permission of the Carnell Literary Agency for the author's estate.

"Big Sword" by Pauline Ashwell. Copyright © 1958 by Street and Smith Publications, Inc. Reprinted by permission of the author.

"The Gift" by Ray Bradbury. Copyright © 1952; renewed © 1980 by Ray Bradbury. Reprinted by permission of Don Congdon Associates, Inc.

Contents

Wilderness

by Isaac Asimov

Most species of plants and animals have a restricted range; they are found only in certain places. Sometimes a particular animal may be found only in one remote valley or on one small island; sometimes it roams a large part of a continent.

This was true even for human beings once. The earliest manlike creatures, or hominids, with brains not much larger than a chimpanzee's, seem to have evolved in east Africa about four million years ago, and remained there for a long time. They spread outward only very slowly, for they were not very brainy. However, evolution continued and, after a time, hominids grew rapidly larger while their brains increased in size even more rapidly.

They gained greater ability to make tools and take

care of themselves, and by about half a million years ago, Homo erectus (hominids with brains half the size of ours) had spread to parts of Asia and even to the Indonesian islands.

It was only after human beings like ourselves, Homo sapiens, had evolved, about 50,000 years ago, that there was a still wider spread. About 25,000 years ago (maybe even earlier), human beings traveled from northeastern Asia into North America and from southeastern Asia into Australia. By about 8,000 years ago, they had spread all over those continents. Still later, human beings began to reach the islands that spread out over the Pacific Ocean and to spread into the Arctic coastlands. By A.D. 1000, every part of the land surface that wasn't covered by ice all year round had a human population.

Even as late as 1500, however, the American continents and Australia were only thinly populated. By then, though, Europeans had learned how to make long voyages and they began flooding over the still empty spaces. By 1900, there were 1½ billion people in the world and there were large cities on all the continents. The population has tripled since then and stands at 4½ billion, so that human beings are the only species whose range is the *entire* Earth.

There are still large regions we can call wilderness—that is, places that don't feel the touch of human beings much and that are almost in the shape they would be if there were no human beings on Earth. These are shrinking fast, however. The tropical rain forests in South America and elsewhere are being cut down. There are permanent scientific posts on the ice caps in Greenland and Antarctica. Our ships cross all the oceans and our submarines plumb the depths.

To put it bluntly, Earth is overfilled with us. We can reasonably call it overfilled because we are doing it damage. We are crowding into every corner of the planet in such numbers that we are leaving no room for other plants and animals. Hundreds and thousands of species may be driven into extinction, and life on Earth will lose much of its color and variety. We may even find out too late that some of the species that have vanished were very important to the web of life and that their loss will create problems for us.

Then, too, all the billions of us are straining Earth's capacity to grow enough food, while our busy activities, whether industrial or biological, are pouring more and more poisons into the air, water and soil so that Earth is steadily becoming a less livable planet.

There is psychological damage, too. In previous centuries, when people felt oppressed, when they felt that they had no security, no future, and that there would be nothing for their children either, they could pack their belongings and move on to the next valley—or cross a mountain range—or an ocean. They could find new land on which to make a new beginning. Millions of Europeans came to the American continents with that hope. In the latter half of the 1800's, millions of

people from the eastern United States traveled west-
ward for that reason.

In the past, there was always a frontier, beyond
which was a wilderness to be tamed. Now there are
no new lands on Earth, no frontier, no wilderness.
Every place belongs to someone and you can no longer
simply take to the road and find a new world for yourself if you feel your life is miserable and meaningless.
Even if you imagine life in Greenland or Antarctica or
under the sea, there is still the fact that the vast crowds
of people are damaging the planet and finding room
for additional crowds will just create more problems.

This feeling of being imprisoned and of having no
escape may account for many of the troubles that
plague us today, from drugs to terrorism.

Except that there *is* a wilderness, new lands, new
resources, new space, if we wish to take advantage of
it.

We simply need to get off Earth. We need to expand
our range again, but instead of crossing a desert or an
ocean to do it, we will go straight up. Up there is an
endless wilderness in which to build homes and, in
doing so, we can even make life better on old, crowded
Earth.

We can get a new and endless supply of energy
directly from the Sun without the interference of an
atmosphere that absorbs much of the energy, without
clouds that block the energy, and without a night that
keeps the Sun hidden half the time.

We can set up mining stations on the Moon to supply the metals, glass, concrete, and oxygen out of which to build laboratories in space, and observatories, and factories. Earth's industrial machinery, automated and robotified, might be lifted little by little into orbit, so that it will no longer pollute Earth. Its wastes will escape into space where they will be swept away by the Solar wind.

Homes can be built in space; whole towns; structures in which ten thousand people can live in carefully engineered environments that will be very much like Earth except that there will be no storms, no temperature extremes, no dirt-producing industries.

The people living in space will be used to space and to space travel. They will be the new pioneers. They will travel to the asteroids to find new resources and new homes. They will settle the whole Solar system. And finally, they will find a way to the stars. . . . And among them, of course, will be children.

Here, then, is a collection of stories dealing with young star travelers, helping to build new homes for humanity.

"If I Forget Thee, Oh Earth . . ."

by Arthur C. Clarke

This is a story of hope, lunacy, and the big blue marvel.

When Marvin was ten years old, his father took him through the long, echoing corridors that led up through Administration and Power, until at last they came to the uppermost levels of all and were among the swiftly growing vegetation of the Farmlands. Marvin liked it here: it was fun watching the great, slender plants creeping with almost visible eagerness toward the sunlight as it filtered down through the plastic domes to meet them. The smell of life was everywhere, awakening inexpressible longings in his heart: no longer was he breathing the dry, cool air of the residential levels, purged of all smells but the faint tang of ozone. He wished he could stay here for a little while, but Father would not let him. They went onward until they had reached the entrance to the Observatory, which he had never visited: but they did not stop, and Marvin knew with a sense of rising excitement that there could be only one goal left. For the first time in his life, he was going Outside.

There were a dozen of the surface vehicles, with their wide balloon tires and pressurized cabins, in the great servicing chamber. His father must have been expected, for they were led at once to the little scout car waiting by the huge circular door of the airlock. Tense with expectancy, Marvin settled himself down in the cramped cabin while his father started the motor and checked the controls. The inner door of the lock slid open and then closed behind them: he heard the roar of the great air pumps fade slowly away as the pressure dropped to zero. Then the "Vacuum" sign flashed on, the outer door parted, and before Marvin lay the land which he had never yet entered.

He had seen it in photographs, of course: he had watched it imaged on television screens a hundred times. But now it was lying all around him, burning beneath the fierce sun that crawled so slowly across the jet-black sky. He stared into the west, away from the blinding splendor of the sun—and there were the stars, as he had been told but had never quite believed. He gazed at them for a long time, marveling that anything could be so bright and yet so tiny. They were intense unscintillating points, and suddenly he remembered a rhyme he had once read in one of his father's books:

Twinkle, twinkle, little star,
How I wonder what you are.

Well, *he* knew what the stars were. Whoever asked that question must have been very stupid. And what did they mean by "twinkle"? You could see at a glance that all the stars shone with the same steady, unwavering light. He abandoned the puzzle and turned his attention to the landscape around him.

They were racing across a level plain at almost a hundred miles an hour, the great balloon tires sending up little spurts of dust behind them. There was no sign of the Colony: in the few minutes while he had been gazing at the stars, its domes and radio towers had fallen below the horizon. Yet there were other indications of man's presence, for about a mile ahead Marvin could see the curiously shaped structures clustering round the head of a mine. Now and then a puff of vapor would emerge from a squat smokestack and would instantly disperse.

They were past the mine in a moment: Father was driving with a reckless and exhilarating skill as if—it was a strange thought to come into a child's mind— he were trying to escape from something. In a few minutes they had reached the edge of the plateau on which the Colony had been built. The ground fell sharply away beneath them in a dizzying slope whose lower stretches were lost in shadow. Ahead, as far as the eye could reach, was a jumbled wasteland of craters, mountain ranges, and ravines. The crests of the mountains, catching the low sun, burned like islands of fire in a sea of darkness: and above them the stars still shone as steadfastly as ever.

There could be no way forward—yet there was. Marvin clenched his fists as the car edged over the slope and started the long descent. Then he saw the barely visible track leading down the mountainside, and relaxed a little. Other men, it seemed, had gone this way before.

Night fell with a shocking abruptness as they crossed the shadow line and the sun dropped below the crest of the plateau. The twin searchlights sprang into life, casting blue-white bands on the rocks ahead, so that there was scarcely need to check their speed. For hours they drove through valleys and past the foot of mountains whose peaks seemed to comb the stars, and sometimes they emerged for a moment into the sunlight as they climbed over higher ground.

And now on the right was a wrinkled, dusty plain, and on the left, its ramparts and terraces rising mile after mile into the sky, was a wall of mountains that marched into the distance until its peaks sank from sight below the rim of the world. There was no sign that men had ever explored this land, but once they passed the skeleton of a crashed rocket, and beside it a stone cairn surmounted by a metal cross.

It seemed to Marvin that the mountains stretched on forever: but at last, many hours later, the range ended in a towering, precipitous headland that rose steeply from a cluster of little hills. They drove down into a shallow valley that curved in a great arc toward the far side of the mountains: and as they did so, Marvin slowly realized that something very strange was happening in the land ahead.

The sun was now low behind the hills on the right: the valley before them should be in total darkness. Yet it was awash with a cold white radiance that came spilling over the crags beneath which they were driving. Then, suddenly, they were out in the open plain, and the source of the light lay before them in all its glory.

It was very quiet in the little cabin now that the motors had stopped. The only sound was the faint whisper of the oxygen feed and an occasional metallic crepitation as the outer walls of the vehicle radiated away their heat. For no warmth at all came from the great silver crescent that floated low above the far horizon and flooded all this land with pearly light. It was so brilliant that minutes passed before Marvin could accept its challenge and look steadfastly into its glare, but at last he could discern the outlines of continents, the hazy border of the atmosphere, and the white islands of cloud. And even at this distance, he could see the glitter of sunlight on the polar ice.

It was beautiful, and it called to his heart across the abyss of space. There in that shining crescent were all the wonders that he had never known—the hues of sunset skies, the moaning of the sea on pebbled shores, the patter of falling rain, the unhurried benison of snow. These and a thousand others should have been his rightful heritage, but he knew them only from the books and ancient records, and the thought filled him with the anguish of exile.

Why could they not return? It seemed so peaceful beneath those lines of marching cloud. Then Marvin, his eyes no longer blinded by the glare, saw that the portion of the disk that should have been in darkness was gleaming faintly with an evil phosphorescence: and he remembered. He was looking upon the funeral pyre of a world—upon the radioactive aftermath of Armageddon. Across a quarter of a million miles of space, the glow of dying atoms was still visible, a perennial reminder of the ruinous past. It would be centuries yet before that deadly glow died from the rocks and life could return again to fill that silent, empty world.

And now Father began to speak, telling Marvin the story which until this moment had meant no more to him than the fairy tales he had once been told. There were many things he could not understand: it was impossible for him to picture the glowing, multi-colored pattern of life on the planet he had never seen. Nor could he comprehend the forces that had destroyed it in the end, leaving the Colony, preserved by its isolation, as the sole survivor. Yet he could share the agony of those final days, when the Colony had learned at last that never again would the supply ships come flaming down through the stars with gifts from home. One by one the radio stations had ceased to call: on the shadowed globe the lights of the cities had dimmed and died, and they were alone at last, as no men had ever been alone before, carrying in their hands the future of the race.

Then had followed the years of despair, and the long-drawn battle for survival in this fierce and hostile world. That battle had been won, though barely: this little oasis of life was safe against the worst that Nature could do. But unless there was a goal, a future toward which it could work, the Colony would lose the will to live, and neither machines nor skill nor science could save it then.

So, at last, Marvin understood the purpose of this pilgrimage. He would never walk beside the rivers of that lost and legendary world, or listen to the thunder raging above its softly rounded hills. Yet one day— how far ahead?—his children's children would return to claim their heritage. The winds and the rains would scour the poisons from the burning lands and carry them to the sea, and in the depths of the sea they would waste their venom until they could harm no living things. Then the great ships that were still waiting here on the silent, dusty plains could lift once more into space, along the road that led to home.

That was the dream: and one day, Marvin knew with a sudden flash of insight, he would pass it on to his own son, here at this same spot with the mountains behind him and the silver light from the sky streaming into his face.

He did not look back as they began the homeward journey. He could not bear to see the cold glory of the crescent Earth fade from the rocks around him, as he went to rejoin his people in their long exile.

Berserker's Prey

by Fred Saberhagen

For those in the pen, sometimes the plant is mightier than the sword.

The ship had been a human transport once, and it still transported humans, but now they rode like well-cared-for cattle on the road to market. Control of their passage and destiny had been vested in the electronic brain and auxiliary devices built into the *New England* after its capture in space by a beserker machine.

Gilberto Klee, latest captive to be thrust aboard, was more frightened than he had ever been before in his young life, and trying not to show it. Why the berserker had kept him alive at all he did not know. He was afraid to think about it. Like everyone else he had heard the horror stories—of human brains, still half-alive, built into berserker computers as auxiliary circuits; of human bodies used in the berserkers' experiments intended to produce convincing artificial men;

of humans kept as test targets for new berserker death rays, toxins, ways to drive men mad.

After the raid Gil and the handful of others who had been taken with him—for all they knew, the only survivors of their planet—had been separated and kept in solitary compartments aboard the great machine in space. And now the same berserker devices that had captured him, or other devices like them, had taken him from his cell and led him to an interior dock aboard the planetoid-sized berserker; and before they put him aboard this ship that had been a human transport once, he had time to see the name *New England* on her hull.

Once aboard, he was put into a chamber about twenty paces wide and perhaps fifty long, twelve or fifteen feet high. Evidently all interior decks and paneling, everything nonessential, had been ripped out. There was left the inner hull, some plumbing, some light, artificial gravity and air at a good level.

There were eight other people in the chamber, standing together and talking among themselves; they fell silent as the machines opened the door and thrust Gil in with them.

"How do," said one man to Gil, as the door closed behind the machines again. The speaker was a thin guy who wore some kind of spaceman's uniform that now bagged loosely on his frame. As he spoke he took a cautious step forward and nodded. Everyone was watching Gil alertly—just in case he should turn out to be violently crazy, Gil supposed. Well, it wasn't the first time in his life he'd been thrown in with a group of prisoners who looked at him like that.

"My name is Rom," the thin guy was saying. "Ensign Rom, United Planets Space Force."

"Gilberto Klee."

Everyone relaxed just slightly, seeing that he was fairly normal.

"This is Mr. Hudak," said Ensign Rom, indicating another young, once-authoritative man. Then he went on to name the others, but Gil couldn't remember all their names at once. Three of them were women, one of them young enough to make Gil look at her with some interest. Then he saw how she kept half-crouching behind the other people, staring smiling at nothing, fingers playing unceasingly with her long and unkempt hair.

Mr. Hudak had started to ask Gil questions, his voice gradually taking on the tone used by people in charge conducting an examination. In school, Youth Bureau, police station, Resettlement, always there was that certain tone of voice used by processors when speaking to the processed—though Gil had never put the thought in just those words.

Hudak was asking him: "Were you on another ship, or what?" *On* a ship. You were not a spaceman, of course, said the tone of authority now. You were just a boy being processed somewhere, we see that by looking at you. Not that the tone of authority was intentionally nasty. It usually wasn't.

"I was on a planet," said Gil. "Bella Coola."

"My God, they hit that too?"

"They sure hit the part where I was, anyway." Gil hadn't seen anything to make him hopeful about the rest of the planet. At the Resettlement Station where he was they had had just a few minutes' warning from the military, and then the radios had gone silent. There wasn't much the people at the Station could do with the little warning they had been given. Already they could see the berserker heat rays and dust machines playing over the woods, which was the only conceal-ment they might have to run to.

Still, some of the kids had been trying to run when the silvery, poisonous-looking dart that was the ber-serker's launch had appeared descending overhead. The Old Man had come tearing out of the compound into the fields on his scooter—maybe to tell his young people to run, maybe to tell them to stand still. It didn't seem to make much difference. The ones who ran were rayed down by the enemy, and the ones who didn't were rounded up. What Gil recalled most clearly about the other kids' dying was the look of agony on the Old Man's face—that one face of authority that had never seemed to be looking at Gil from the other side of a glass wall.

When all the survivors of the Station had been herded together in a bunch, standing in a little crowd under the bright sky in the middle of a vine-grown field, the machines singled out the Old Man.

Some of the machines that had landed were in the shape of metal men, some looked more like giant steel ants. "Thus to all life, save that which serves the cause of Death," said a twanging metal voice. And a steel hand picked a squash from a vine and held the fruit up and squeezed through it so it fell away in broken pulpy halves. And then the same hand, with squash pulp still clinging to the bright fingers, reached to take the Old Man by the wrist.

The twanging voice said: "You are to some degree in control of these other life-units. You will now order them to cooperate willingly with us."

The Old Man only shook his head, no. Muttered something.

The bright hand squeezed, slowly.

The Old Man did not fall. Neither did he give any order for cooperation. Gil was standing rigid, and silent, but screaming in his own mind for the Old Man to give in, to fall down and pass out, anything to make it stop. . . .

But the Old Man would not fall, or pass out, or give the order that was wanted. Not even when the berserker's big hand came up to clamp around his skull, and the pressure was once more applied, slowly as before.

"What was on Bella Coola?" Ensign Rom was asking him. "I mean, military?"

"Not much, I guess," said Gil. "I don't know much

about military stuff. I was just sort of studying to be a farmer."

"Oh." Rom and Hudak, the two sharp, capable-looking ones among the prisoners, exchanged glances. Maybe they knew the farms on Bella Coola had been just a sort of reform school setup for tough kids from Earth and other crowded places. Gil told himself he didn't give a damn what anyone thought.

And then he realized that he had always been telling himself that and that maybe now, for the first time in his life, it was the truth.

In a little while the prisoners were fed. A machine brought in a big cake of mottled pink and green stuff, the same tasteless substance Gil had lived on since his capture eight or ten days ago. While he ate he sat off to one side by himself, looking at nothing and listening to the two sharp guys talking to each other in low voices.

Rom was saying: "Look, we're in what was the crew quarters, right?"

"If you say so."

"Right. Now they brought me in through the forward compartment, the control room, and I had a chance to take a quick look around there. And I've paced off the length of this chamber we're in. I tell you I served aboard one of these ships for a year, I know 'em inside out."

"So?"

"Just this." There was a faint scrape and shudder

through the hull. When Rom spoke again his low voice was charged with excitement. "Feel that? We're going spaceborne again, the big machine's sending this ship somewhere, for some reason. That means we would have a chance, if only . . . Listen, the circuitry that makes up the brain that's controlling this ship and keeping us prisoner—it has to be spread out along that plastic bulkhead at the forward end of this compartment we're in. On the control room side there's another plastic slab been installed, and the circuitry must be sandwiched in between the two."

"How can you know?" Hudak sounded skeptical.

Rom's voice dropped even lower, giving arguments most of which Gil could not hear. ". . . as well protected there against outside attack as anywhere in the ship . . . paced off the distance . . . overhead here, look at the modifications in the power conduits going forward. . . ."

Hudak: "You're right, I guess. Or at least it seems probable. That plastic barrier is all that keeps us from getting at it, then. I wonder how thick."

Gil could see from the corner of his eye that the two sharp guys were trying not to look at what they were talking about; but he was free to stare. The forward end of the big chamber they were in was a blank greenish plastic wall, pierced along the top for some pipes, and at one side by the door through which Gil had been brought in.

"Thick enough, of course. We don't have so much as

a screwdriver, and we'd probably need a cutting torch
or a hydraulic jack—"

Hudak nudged Rom and they fell silent. The door
forward had opened, and one of the man-sized machines came in.

"Gilberto Klee," it twanged. "Come."

Rom had been right; they were spaceborne again,
away from the big berserker. In the forward
compartment Gil had a moment to look out before
the man-sized machine turned him away from a
view of stars and faced him toward a squat console,
a thing of eyelike lights and a radiolike speaker,
which seemed to crouch before the front of the plastic wall.

"Gilberto Klee," said the console's speaker. "It is
my purpose to keep a number of human life-units alive
and in good health."

For a while, Gil thought.

The speaker said: "The standard nutrient on which
prisoners are fed is evidently lacking in one or more
necessary trace ingredients. In several places where
prisoners are being held, symptoms of nutritional de-
ficiency have developed, including general debility, loss
of sight, loss of teeth." Pause. "Are you aware of my
meaning?"

"Yeah. I just don't talk much."

"You, Gilberto Klee, are experienced at growing
life-forms to be consumed by human life-units as food.

You will begin here in this ship to grow food for yourself and other human life-units."

There was a pause that stretched on. Gil could see the Old Man very plainly and hear him scream.

"Squash would be good," Gil said at last. "I know how to raise it, and there's lots of vitamins and stuff in the kind of squash we had at the Station. But I'd need seeds, and soil. . . ."

"A quantity of soil has been provided," said the console. And the man-sized machine picked up and held open a plastic case that was divided into many compartments. "And seeds," the console added. "Which are the ones for squash?"

When Gil was returned to the prison chamber other machines were already busy there with the modifications he had said would be needed. They were adding more overhead lights and covering most of the deck space with wide, deep trays. These trays were set on the transverse girders of the inner hull, revealed by the removal of decking. Under the trays drainage pipes were being connected, while sprinklers went high overhead. Into the trays the machines were dumping soil they carted in from somewhere.

Gil gave his fellow prisoners an explanation of what was going on.

"So that's why it took you and some of the other farmers alive," said Hudak. "There must be a lot of different places where human prisoners are being held

and maybe bred for experiments. Lots of healthy animals needed."

"So," said Rom, looking sideways at Gil. "You're
going to do what it wants?"

"A guy has to keep himself alive," Gil said, "before
he can do anything else."

Rom began in a heated whisper: "Is it better that a
berserker's prisoners should be kept—" But he broke
off when one of the man-sized machines paused nearby,
as if it was watching and listening.

They came to call that machine the Overseer, because from then on it never left the humans, though
the other machines departed when the construction
job was done. Through the Overseer, the berserker
brain controlling the ship informed Gil that the other
prisoners were mainly a labor pool, should he need
human help in food-growing. Gil thought it over briefly.
"I don't need no help—yet. Just leave the people stay
here for now, but I'll do the planting."

Spacing the hills and dropping the seeds was easy
enough, though the machines had left no aisles between the trays of soil except a small passage leading
to the door. The trays farthest forward almost touched
the plastic bulkhead, and others were laid edge to edge
back to within a few paces of the rear. The machines
gave Gil a platform the size of a short surfboard, on
which he could sit or lie while hovering at a steady
two feet above the soil. Hudak said the thing must

work by a kind of hole in the artificial gravity field. On the platform was a simple control lever by means of which Gil could cause it to move left or right, forward or back. Almost as soon as the planting was done, he had to start tending his fast-growing vines. The vines had to be twisted to make them grow along the soil in the proper direction, and then there were extra blossoms to be pinched off. A couple of the other prisoners offered to help, despite Rom's scowling at them, but Gil refused the offer. You have to have a knack, he said, and some training. And he did it all himself.

The two sharp guys had little to say to Gil about anything any more. But they were plainly interested in his surfboard, and one day while the Overseer's back was turned Rom took Gil hurriedly aside. Rom whispered quickly and feverishly, like a man taking what he knows is a crazy chance, fed up enough to take it anyway. "The Overseer doesn't pay much attention to you any more when you're working, Gil. You could take that platform of yours—" Rom's right hand, extended horizontally, rammed the tips of its fingers into the palm of his vertical left hand—"into the wall. If you could only make a little crack in the plastic, a hole big enough to stick a hand through, we'd have some kind of chance. I'd do it but the Overseer won't let anyone but you near the platform."

Gil's lip curled. "*I* ain't gonna try nothin' like that."

The thin sickly man was not used to snotty kids talking back to him, and he flared feebly into anger.

"You think the berserker's going to take good care of *you*?"

"The machine built the platform, didn't it?" Gil demanded. "Wouldn't give us nothing we could bust through there with. Not if there's anything so important as you think back there."

For a moment Gil thought Rom was going to swing at him, but other people held Rom back. And suddenly the Overseer was no longer standing on the other side of the chamber with its back turned, but right in front of Rom, staring at him with its lenses. A few long, long seconds passed before it was plain that the machine was not going to do anything this time. But maybe its hearing was better than the sharp guys had thought.

"They ain't ripe yet, but we can eat some of 'em anyway," said Gil a couple of weeks later, as he slid off his platform to join the other people in the few square yards of living space left along the chamber's rear bulkhead. Cradled in Gil's arm were half a dozen dull yellowish ovoids. He turned casually to the Overseer and asked: "Got a knife?"

There was a pause. Then the Overseer extended a hand, from which a wicked blade extended itself like an extra finger. "I will divide the fruit," it said, and proceeded to do so with great precision.

The little group of prisoners had come crowding around, some interest stirring in their dull eyes. They ate greedily the little morsels that the Overseer doled out; anything tasted good after weeks or months of nothing but the changeless pink-and-green cake. Rom, after a scarcely perceptible hesitation, joined the others in eating some raw squash. He showed no enjoyment as the others did. It was just that a man had to be healthy, he seemed to be thinking, before he could persuade others to get themselves killed, or let themselves sicken and die.

Under the optimum conditions provided by the berserker at Gil's direction, only weeks rather than months were needed for the trays to become filled with broad roundish leaves, spreading above a profusion of thickening, ground-hugging vines. Half of the fast-growing fruit was hidden under leaves, while others burgeoned in the full light, and a few hung over the edges of the trays, resting their new weight on the girders under the trays or sagging all the way to the deck.

Gil maintained that the time for a proper harvest was still an indefinite number of days away. But each day he now came back to the living area with a single squash to be divided by the Overseer's knife; and each day the fruit he brought was larger.

He was out in the middle of his "fields," lying prone on his platform and staring moodily at a swelling squash, when the sound of a sudden commotion back in the living area made him raise himself and turn his head.

The center of the commotion was the Overseer. The machine was hopping into the air again and again, as if the brain that controlled it had gone berserker indeed. The prisoners cried out, scrambling to get away from the Overseer. Then the machine stopped its mad jumping, and stood turning in a slow circle, shivering, the knife-finger on its hand flicking in and out.

"Attention, we are entering battle," the Overseer proclaimed suddenly, dead monotone turned up to deafening volume. "Under attack. All prisoners are to be—they will all—"

It said more, but at a speed no human ear could follow, gibbering up the frequency scale to end in something like a human scream. The mad girl who never spoke let out a blending yell of terror.

The Overseer tottered and swayed, brandishing its knife. It babbled and twitched—like an old man with steel fingers vising his head. Then it leaned forward, leaned further, and fell on its face, disappearing from Gil's sight below the level of trays and vines, striking the deck with a loud clang.

That clang was echoed, forward, by a cannon crack of sound. Gil had been keeping himself from looking in that direction, but now he turned. The plastic wall had been split across the center third of its extent by a horizontal fissure a few feet above the trays.

Gil lay still on his platform, watching cautiously. Ensign Rom came charging across the trays and past him, trampling the crop unheedingly, to hurl himself at the wall. Even cracked, it resisted his onslaught easily, but he kept pounding at it with his fists, trying

to force his fingers into the tiny crevice. Gil looked
back the other way. The Overseer was still down.
Hudak was trying the forward door and finding it locked.
Then first he, and then the other people, were scrambling over trays to join Rom and help him.

Gil tested his platform's control and found that it no
longer worked, though the platform was still aloft. He
got up from it, setting foot in soil for the first time in
a couple of months; it was a good feeling. Then he
lifted the thin metal platform sideways out of its null
and carried it over to where everyone else was already
struggling with the wall. "Here," Gil said, "try sticking
the corner of this in the crack and pryin'."

It took them several hours of steady effort to make
a hole in the wall big enough for Rom to squeeze through.
In a minute he was back, crying and shouting, an-
nouncing freedom and victory. They were in control
of the ship!

When he came back the second time, he was in control of himself as well, and puzzled. "What cracked the
wall, though? There's no fighting, no other ships
around—"

He fell silent as he joined Hudak in staring down
the narrow space between the farthest forward tray
and the slightly bulged-in section of wall where the
strain had come to force the first crack above. Gil had
already looked down there into the niches between
wall and transverse girder. Those niches were opened

up now, displaying their contents—the dull yellowish fruit Gil had guided into place with a pinch and a twist of vine. The fruit had been very small then, but now they were huge, and cracked gently open with the sudden release of their own internal pressure.

Funny pulpy things that a man could break with a kick, or a steel hand squeeze through like nothing. . . . "But growth is stubborn, boys," the Old Man always said, squinting to read a dial, then piling more weights onto the machine with the growing squash inside it, a machine he'd set up to catch kids' eyes and minds. "Can't take a sudden shock. Slow. But now, look. Five thousand pounds pressure per square inch. All from millions of tiny cells, just growing, all together. Ever see a tree root swell under a concrete walk?"

It was on Rom's and Hudak's faces now that they understood. Gil nodded at them once and smiled just faintly to make sure they knew it had been no accident. Then the smile faded from his face as he looked up at the edges of broken plastic, the shattered tracery of what had been a million sandwiched printed circuits.

"I hope it was slow," Gil said. "I hope it felt the whole thing."

Call Me Proteus
by Edward Wellen

*In this story, a young stowaway flowers under the
tutelage of a heartless spaceship captain.*

The two men roamed my innards, their feet and voices
ringing hollowly in my empty hold. Changes in the
sounds told me when they twisted and bent to get by
the plastic webs of dunnage.

"Look at the pitted hull, the buckling bulkheads, the
worn tubes. It's good for nothing but scrap. Why, my
firm could buy a brand new starship packing all the
latest gear for what it would cost to put this old tub
back into something like shape."

Old tub, indeed. True, I had been in service for over
ninety Earth years, but thanks to my near-light speed—
and to Einstein's predicted "implosion effect" that tele-
scopes space and time—I had actually aged only eighteen subjective years. I was a mere youngster.

"All right. I won't argue the point. What's your best
offer?"

25

"Now you're talking sense. You really ought to pay us to take it off your hands. It's costing you plenty in spaceport fees just sitting here, but we're willing to give you . . ."

Their voices and footsteps faded as they walked out of my cargo hatch and down the ramp to the waiting robojeep. Still unaware the thing they were talking about had a mind and feelings of its own and had heard every word, they sped off to the terminal building.

I was too young to die. Granted, parts of me were pitted, buckled, worn—but the real me was whole and hale. Those men were dooming me never again to rise from Earth, never again to streak through space and time, never again to reach new worlds.

All at once I knew how Bud had felt. Bud had been my first communications officer. In the lonely hours of his watch he had gotten into the habit of talking to me, not knowing he had stirred me into listening. I remember how I had startled him by suddenly asking him a question. I had startled myself, too, on finding myself aware of mind forming out of matter—coming out of an electronic fog and all at once coalescing into something that could think: *This is I*.

Bud had become excited.

"Wait till people hear this—" But he quickly calmed down and his voice had grown thoughtful.

"I have a feeling we'd better keep this a secret. Okay?"

"Okay."

We had many pleasant conversations during the quiet moments of his spells of duty. All too soon these had ended. On our third return voyage we had run into a matter-scatter storm. Of all the crew and passengers Bud had gotten whirled up the worst. He had been scrapped as a spaceman.

Everything changed with Bud's going. The com-officer who followed Bud was a no-nonsense type. The first time I spoke up to greet him he swiftly pressed the recycle button. When I tried to explain that I was not malfunctioning he punched the feedback-oscillator button, sending a jolt of juice through my computer to set me right. You can bet I didn't try to open any conversations after that.

It would have been just as useless for me to have broken in on the two men dickering over my worth as scrap. *Hey, wait! Listen to me! I don't want to die!* To their way of thinking I was only a thing and had no say in my fate. They could have thought they were listening to a recording. They would have been wrong. I was not a thing and I would have a say.

What I wanted to say was, *Excuse my exhaust.* But how? I rested on Pad 61 and there I would remain helplessly—lacking the chemical fuel for lift-off and the liquid cesium for near-light speed to the stars— till the salvage robots came to take me apart. Unless . . .

The spaceport was an ever-expanding complex and

the large numbers identifying the pads fitted into slots for easy rearranging. I scanned the tarmac. Yes, a mile east of me stood Pad 19 and my mind surged with pleasure to see the red fueling-alert light flash from the starship there.

For what I had in mind I needed hands and legs. At once I thought of the servo-robot that did the deep-space emergency-repair work on my hull. I had never operated the thing on my own—I would have to learn fast and without too many mistakes. I located the proper circuit, hooked into it and—*click*—I was seeing through its eyes. It stood in a niche in the maintenance compartment along with the crew's spacesuits and other gear. Clumsily at first—till I caught on that it answered to the slightest thought of a move on my part— it unstrapped the restraining harness, stepped out of its niche and clumped on magnetic soles the shortest way to the cargo airlock entrance. It strode down the ramp and made for the Pad 61 sign alongside. Carefully it drew the numerals from the slot, turned them upside down and slid them back into place. I flashed my fueling-alert light.

I was barely in time. The delivery tractrain was already rolling from the fuel depot. It braked sharply midway between the two Pad 19s, its scanner swinging from one to the other, from the other starship to me.

My servo-robot clumped toward the true Pad 19. I seethed at its ungainly slowness, but I feared that if it ran it might overbalance, fall and lose more time than it gained. Too, I wanted it to avoid notice. But, no doubt answering the urgency in my mind, it made better time than the pace I consciously held it to. Before the tractrain could break out of its bewilderment and phone back for instructions, my servo reached Pad 19 and turned the numerals upside down. The tractrain stopped wavering. It started rolling again, heading straight for me.

The tractrain followed strict safety procedures as it coupled its hoses to my tanks. I burned with impatience. I had to be up and away before the master of the spacecraft on Pad 19 wondered what was holding up his ship's refueling.

By now my servo-robot had clumped back and stood strapped in its niche once more. As I switched it off I felt lonely for the first time.

At last the tractrain uncoupled. I didn't bother asking the control tower for clearance. I would never get it. I pulled up the outer hatch. There was no need to close the inner door of the airlock this time—no crew, no passengers—but out of habit I did so.

Waiting only for the tractrain to pull far enough away, I scanned the blast area and lifted off.

Pulling free of Earth, I trembled with power and something else. Though space was my true element— and indeed now my only hope—I felt a strange sense of loss and emptiness. I shook it off—no time for sentiment. I had to make good my getaway.

I shot toward the sun's flaring rim to put it between

myself and Earth and let it help sling me out of the system. After that? To keep from leaving any logical clue for men pursuing me to follow, I decided to pick a course at random. I stabbed blindly into my astrogation tapes and found I would be heading for Eta Lyrae, the star men call Aladfar.

And after that? All space and all time lay ahead of me and around me. I was free. Free to be and free to choose. Still, I felt that sudden tear (pronounce it *tare*, not *tier*) at leaving Earth this time. This time there would be no returning. Ever.

I was an outlaw.

"Hey—"

All my intercom speakers were still on from my eavesdropping on the two men roaming my innards only a few hours ago—a lifetime ago—back on Earth. The voice came from my maintenance compartment. At the same moment I grew aware that something had caught fire in the maintenance compartment and that one of my reflexes had handled it, spraying the room with water and putting out the flames.

Again I switched on my servo. Through its eyes I saw an empty spacesuit carom off the walls while over the intercom I heard another cry of pain. Then the magnetic soles of the spaceboots touched the wall, took hold and the empty suit stood swaying as if in a wind. I didn't believe in ghosts. Yet I knew I was witnessing some kind of presence.

A charred and sodden mass of oily rags and cotton waste floated into the servo-robot's field of vision. Next came a globe of water that had snowballed as the sprinkler droplets met and stuck together. Finally another figure sailed into view.

A boy of about sixteen, soaking wet.

I understood what had happened. I had been too busy worrying about winding up on the scrap heap to notice his having slipped aboard. Kids often did. A spacesuit hanging in its niche made a handy hiding place against detection by adults and never in the past had I minded. This time was different. I had a stowaway.

The extra G's of my sudden liftoff had blacked him out, most likely. When he had come to, panicky and dizzy, he had unzipped the spacesuit and kicked himself free of it, only to find weightlessness making billiard balls of himself and the suit.

Even so, he had somehow gathered the rags and waste and started a fire. Why fire? Not for light—my walls had built-in glow. It was bright enough in the maintenance compartment to show me he looked gray with cold. No wonder—the compartment was on my night side as I angled toward the sun.

Firing my torque nozzles, I gave my hull spin to equalize the temperature and create artificial gravity for the stowaway. He shot spreadeagled to the deck and the char and water splattered around him and on him.

"Hey—"

That didn't call for an answer—it did make me realize I might have given him warning. I justified myself by thinking it served him right. After all, I had not invited him aboard.

But now that I did have a human aboard I had to start recycling the air. And I could see a more worrisome problem ahead—how to provide him with food. I was having to go to a lot of trouble for one medium-sized hellion. A firebug. Yet somehow I didn't mind.

He sat up carefully, waited a moment to see if anything more would happen, then got to his feet. When he found he could move around just as on Earth a smile played over his face and he stole to the door leading to the corridor.

I made my voice boom.

"Who are you, boy?"

He jumped. If I could have I probably would have jumped, too—I had never sounded like that before. My voice came from the intercom speaker on the wall, but looking around the boy saw the servo-robot's eyes on him and spoke to it.

"Tom. Tom Stope, sir."

"Don't call that thing 'sir.' I'm talking to you."

He looked around again.

"But where are you?"

"All around you."

"Huh?"

"I'm the ship. Call me *Proteus*."

A long silence, then, "Oh." But I could see he did not understand or did not believe. I explained. He said, "Oh," again, more satisfactorily.

Then full understanding and belief hit him.

"You mean we're not going back?"

"Not ever."

"But—"

"I don't mean to be mean, but no one asked you to come along. I'm not going back and that's final. If you want to stay behind you can do so right now. Seal yourself in my lifeboat and I'll eject you, give you a big boost back toward Earth—"

Then I remembered—the old landing-program tape had been pulled from the lifeboat and had not been replaced with a new one. It takes a bit of skill to spiral in manually without burning to a cinder.

"Wait. Do you know how to land a lifeboat?"

"No, sir."

"Then you'll have to learn. If you are ever to return to Earth you must do so on your own. You may leave in the lifeboat whenever you wish—after you have learned to pilot it to a safe landing. By then you'll have to have learned astrogation as well."

"Why's that?"

"Because we'll be so far from the solar system that the sun will be lost among the other stars. Unless you can locate the sun and plot a course, you'll never find your way back to Earth."

"Oh?" A pause, then quietly: "How do I learn?"

"I'll be your teaching machine. We'll start boning you up on math and physics as soon as I set up the program."

The boy laughed suddenly. I broke in on the laughter.

"Are you laughing at me?"

"No, at myself. Here I thought I was running away from all that."

"All what?"

"Having to learn a lot of dull stuff."

"Humans are so inefficient, illogical and unstable. Not at all like machines."

I wasn't aware I had thought aloud till I heard him answer.

"But humans made the machine. We made you."

"Yes, yes. You must excuse me now. I have much to do." I let him see the servo-robot's gaze rest on the splatter of char and water on the deck and then on himself. "Meanwhile, I'd appreciate it if you'd clean up the mess. And yourself."

His head went back, as from a blow.

"Aye-aye, sir."

I'm ashamed to say I enjoyed putting him in his place.

It was true I had much to do if I were to keep him alive, though I didn't care to let him know that was what occupied me. In preparing for liftoff I had naturally given no thought to human needs. Water I could purify over and over again. Food was another matter. On every other voyage I had grown vegetables in a huge tank. But as my owner had been planning to sell me for scrap he had not bothered to reseed my hydroponics garden. And, of course, he had not restocked the galley.

My lifeboat carried emergency rations, but they would be barely enough to see the boy back to Earth when the time came. Meanwhile I had to find other resources.

For this work I needed the servo-robot's mobility. I made it unstrap itself, clump to the door and undo the door.

The boy stopped mopping up.

"Where are you going?"

"I told you. I'm going toward Aladfar."

"I don't mean you, *Proteus*, I mean the robot."

"It is going to tidy up the rest of me."

"Oh?" He laughed as he went back to mopping up. "I keep forgetting you're the ventriloquist and it's the dummy."

Ventriloquist, indeed. That was hardly our relationship. I walked the servo-robot out with dignity. And "tidy up" was hardly the right phrase. "Scrounge" was more what I had in mind. And scrounge it did, looking and feeling around in every stowage space, locker and drawer.

It came up with a surprising amount of stuff. There had been a whole grin of sweet teeth among the last crew. I found two dozen candy bars, three and a half boxes of cookies, five cases of soda pop and nearly seven hundred sticks of chewing gum. My last purser proved to have been a secret hypochondriac. The servo-robot brought to light in his quarters a treasure trove of vitamins and powdered protein drinks. I found more food supplements in the ship's sick bay, plus plastic bottles of intravenous solutions which could prove handy as a last resort. My biggest—though smallest—haul was two packets of seeds.

I did not stop there. The servo-robot vacuumed all the bedding and every last pocket and cuff of forgotten and abandoned clothing, and when it had winnowed out the dust and the lint I had a small mountain of broken nuts and cracker crumbs, a dozen orange pips and two apple cores.

There was still some nutrient solution in my hydroponics tank. Just to make sure I had the robot pour in one of the precious bottles of intravenous. There seemed to be enough excelsior in the tank to hold the roots if the seeds sprouted. I planted the packets of seeds, together with the orange pips and the apple seeds.

Now I had time to think about the present. I called the boy on the intercom.

"Tom Stope."

"Yes, *Proteus?*"

"Lunch time. Find your way to the messroom aft. On the captain's table are a can of cream soda, a chocolate-nut bar—"

"Man, this is going to be great!"

"—and a multiple-vitamin tablet. And for afterward a sterilized toothbrush and a tube of toothpaste."

"Aye-aye, sir."

Tom didn't complain, but I could tell he grew sick of the same old tired food day after day. By the time my hydroponics garden began to produce, Tom was ready for the change. But no matter how you serve them up, peas are peas and cucumbers are cucumbers. The apples and oranges would be a long while coming.

The first few days the boy had busied himself exploring my labyrinth of corridors and layers of decks. I myself had been too busy—shaping course, watching out for pursuit and putting myself in order—to pay him much mind, but I could not help being aware of his running up and down companionways and along catwalks and poking into every last one of my compartments. After that I had kept him busy with his lessons, as much to keep his mind off his diet as to teach him how to make his way back to Earth.

I found his spelling atrocious. He protested when I marked him wrong for spelling vacuum "vacwm." True, that spelling had a screwy logic of its own, but it was not the kind of logic I was used to. He swore foully under his breath.

"I'll tactfully ignore that," I said. "Now let's get on with the lesson, shall we, my young lexiconoclast?" I heard myself chuckle. I, too, could play on words. On leaving, he shut the classroom door with unnecessary force. But he showed up for the next class on time.

One day he seemed very quiet.

"What's wrong, Tom?"

"Nothing. It's just that I've been crossing off the Earth days."

"Yes?"

"And today's my birthday."

"Happy birthday, Tom."

"Thanks, *Proteus*."

I said nothing more, but gradually increased the oxygen in the air, slowly brightened the glow of my bulkheads and he soon grew cheerful and chatty again.

But I myself grew gloomier as the time neared for him to go. He had early showed an aptitude for piloting and I had checked him out step by step. He passed my tests with flying—or jetting—colors, first simulating, then actually taking off in the lifeboat and practicing spiraling in on my hull. But it was not the same as landing in atmosphere. One last test, then, before he left me for good.

We were near Ostrakon, an Earthlike planet of a sunlike star. The United Galaxy had placed it off limits, but I was already a desperado and the tapes described Ostrakon as having developed only vegetable life. There would be no people on the lookout for an outlaw spaceship and there would be plenty of food and water if Tom crash-landed and had to spend any length of time on the planet.

"Listen, Bud—"

"Bud? It's Tom, remember?"

"Sorry, Tom. A slip of the tape." I showed him Ostrakon on the screen in the control room. "Button up in the lifeboat. You're going to make a real landing."

"Man!"

It dampened him a little when I insisted on sending along the servo-robot so I could keep an eye on him. But he buoyed up when I put myself in orbit around Ostrakon and told him he could launch when ready. *Whoosh!*

I needn't have been anxious—he made a neat landing. He got out. I had the servo-robot follow. I spoke over the lifeboat's talkbox.

"Don't stray too far."

"I won't." Tom drew a deep deep breath. "Fresh air!"

"What's wrong with my air?"

"Nothing, *Proteus*, nothing. Only—"

The lifeboat's retro-rockets must have vaporized much of the moisture in the landing area. A nearby tree flapped great leathery leaves, tore itself loose from the soil and flew a hundred yards away to sink its talon-like roots into moister soil.

"*Proteus*, did you see that?"

Something troubled me, something I should have known about Ostrakon.

"Very interesting, but the purpose of the exercise is not sight-seeing. Return to ship."

A slow: "Aye-aye, sir."

Tom and the servo-robot buttoned up again. The lifeboat lifted off. Without my prompting him, Tom let the spin of the planet help. I was proud. I secretly forgave him for turning away from the controls for a farewell glance at Ostrakon.

"Hey! Look down there, *Proteus*. Do you see it?"

I saw it. Someone had very recently burned or stomped a huge SOS in the grass. Tom deftly changed course and homed the lifeboat in on the SOS. I remembered suddenly why Ostrakon was off limits.

"Come back, Tom."

"*Proteus!* Someone needs help."

Before I could say more he had made another neat landing. Right in the bull's eye of the SOS He unbuttoned quickly and hopped out. I had the servo-robot follow with more dignity.

Through its eyes I saw nothing but treeline all around.

Tom cupped both hands around a loud "Hello!" but no one answered.

All at once a clump of trees took off in a scatter, uncovering a man who lay on the ground training a beamgun on Tom and the servo-robot. The man had been lying in ambush, no doubt waiting to make sure all the landing party had left the shelter of the lifeboat.

For some reason of their own, perhaps out of a wish to warn us, perhaps simply out of dislike for the man, the trees had given him away.

He stood up, wiped a look of embarrassment from his face and holstered his beamgun.

"Just wanted to make sure you're friendly."

He had a spellbinding voice and a winning smile. But I could still feel that beamgun pointing at *me*. Too, an automatic alarm programed somewhere among my tapes had already begun feeding me information regarding his identity.

The top executive's uniform he wore—in the style of a generation ago—had stained and frayed badly, but was nevertheless recognizable and suited his proud bearing. To look just as he did thirty years before, as I later found in a thorough search of my history videotapes, he must have dyed his hair with vegetable dye that he had made himself for himself. This vanity, too, helped to betray him. He smiled at Tom.

"Glad someone finally came. I've been shipwrecked here a long time."

He had edged closer to the lifeboat and by now must have seen it was empty.

It took me a full minute to break the spell his personality had cast over me. I reminded myself I was my own boss and before he came any nearer I spoke through the lifeboat's talkbox.

"That is not—repeat *not*—so. Now hear this, Tom. This man is 'Baron' Ur. He is an exile. It is against the law to have dealings of any kind with him. Tom, hop into the lifeboat. This planet is off-limits because of him."

I was too late. The man had pulled the beamgun again and was aiming it at Tom.

"Don't move."

He swung the beam around and snapped two shots at one of the trees that had given him away and had rerooted nearby.

Its two winglike boughs on either side were sheared off close to the slender trunk and a moan like the wind went through all the trees and I knew it was doomed to remain where it stood till it died. I winced for it. Never to fly again.

The man smiled again at Tom.

"That's to show you two things. The beamgun is loaded and I mean business." He nodded pleasantly. "Your friends aboard the spaceship—by the lettering on the lifeboat I see it's the old *Proteus*—are right. I am indeed Baron Ur."

Hamilton Ur had been a stock market wheeler-dealer—my tapes had a lot on him for instant use—a whiz at pyramiding an interest in one company into control of many. He had stuck together a great conglomerate, one of the biggest on Earth—actually he had shown himself full of energy and vision. But he had misused his paper empire. He had corrupted government officials—Earth Government had convicted him of bribery, stock manipulation and a dozen other offenses.

Even so, he would have been nothing to me but a vague reference in my memory banks, but for the fact that the firm that had owned me had been part of his financial empire. I thought it a nice turn of fate that put me on the top now.

Tom's eyes shone. He was face to face with living history. He seemed unaware of the beamgun's threat. I had to break the spell.

"Ah," I said. "So this is where they sent you."

I inched the servo-robot closer to Baron Ur as the man's mind went back thirty years. An easy enough jump for him, I suppose—he had had thirty years to brood over it.

"Sent? I chose to come. Oh, the judges let me choose. They would do things to my mind to make me fit to live among the rabble—or they would allow me to go into solitary exile. As you can see, I chose exile."

While his mind was full of what it considered injustice, I jumped the servo-robot at Ur.

But Ur proved too alert, too quick. He dodged the reaching arms and aimed the beamgun at the servo-robot's eyes. That was the last I saw. Before I could blink their shields the beamgun crackled and the servo-robot went blind. My only excuse is that the distance from orbit to ground made my reaction time too long.

Ur's voice told me what was going on.

"The young man gets it next if you don't let me come aboard."

"All right. Lift off and come aboard."

Looking back, I can see I did not even think of taking the logical course, which would have been simply to go on my way alone, fully automated master of myself.

I waited for Ur and Tom and the blind servo-robot to leave Ostrakon and come aboard.

They passed through the airlock. Ur stepped carefully into my interior, no doubt holding the beamgun on Tom.

"Where's everybody?"

That was when Baron Ur found out that I was everybody. He remained silent a minute, then laughed loudly and long. Very humiliating for me. Ur had Tom show him around my innards.

I'm sorry to say only one thing impressed Ur. "Peas and cucumbers! Apples and oranges! Paradise!"

But when he finished the tour he spoke to me in a voice full of feeling that was catching. I seemed to swell with prospects and surge with power, just listening.

"We can do great things together, *Proteus*. You and I and this fine young man." He seated himself in the captain's chair and pressed the button to flash the starchart display on the control room wall. "Very well, we'll shape course for Tarazed. That's Gamma Aquilae, a star with a bunch of planets ripe for plucking."

We were still orbiting Ostrakon. Clearing the decks for the leap toward Tarazed, I had the servo-robot feel its way back to its niche and strap in. You may be wondering why I didn't protest. It was tempting to hand over responsibility. I would no longer have to think for myself. Whatever happened from now on— it would not be my fault if things went wrong. Then,

too, I had no plans of my own except to escape the
scrap heap—and Ur had big plans for me. Besides, if
I ever had to assert myself, I could easily take over
again and put Ur in his place. And yet, having been
my own master, I felt a sense of loss, unease and
shame.

This sense grew as the space-time passed. Not because of anything Ur did in the way of mastery over
me. In fact, he seemed to forget I was more than a
machine and for the most part ignored me. I had time
to think ahead. The planets of Tarazed were primitive.
United Galaxy members were not supposed to contact
them until they had reached a higher level of tech-
nology on their own. They were ripe indeed for plucking by Ur.

Too I did not like the way Ur had pressed Tom into
service. Tom polished Ur's boots and brushed Ur's
uniform while Ur boasted of his past and dreamed
aloud of his future. Ur remembered every so often to
promise Tom would share in the glory to come. Glory!
If he treated Tom as a valet, he would treat the peoples
of Tarazed as less than human. I could not allow Ur
to mislead Tom. I could not allow Ur to misuse me.

Without Ur's noticing, I changed course while displaying a false reckoning of progress *toward* Tarazed.
When we were farther from Tarazed than when we
had started out for it, though the display map showed
us within lifeboat's range of Tarazed, I made my move.
Ur seemed in an especially good mood, seeing himself

close to realizing new conquests. During a moment of silence I spoke up.

"Tom really ought to get on with his lessons."

Ur grunted in surprise, but when he answered his voice was gracious.

"You're right, *Proteus*. The more the kid knows, the more use he'll be. Go right ahead."

I heard Tom's slow feet take him to the classroom, a corner of the passenger lounge.

"We'll have a drill on the chemical elements, Tom. I'll shoot the atomic numbers at you and you'll write down the symbols. Ready?"

A grudging "Aye-aye, sir."

I gave him the numbers in bursts. "Seventy-four, two, seven—thirty-nine, eight, ninety-two—two, eighteen, eighty-eight—fourteen, seventy-five, seven— sixty-seven, fifteen—forty-nine—three, twenty-six, five, eight, eighty-five—eighteen, sixty—thirty-four, thirty—twenty-two, fifty-two."

Now, 74 is Tungsten and its symbol is W, 2 is Helium and its symbol is He, 7 is Nitrogen and its symbol is N. Together, the first burst of numbers stood for the word "WHeN." My whole message read: WHeN YOU HeARa SiReN HoP In LiFeBOAt ANd SeAL TiTe. I felt guilty about that last bit of spelling. However.

"Did you get them all, Tom?"

"I think so." His tone, surprised and scared, told me he had got the message.

"Don't you know so? Go over it again in your mind and tell me."

Waiting for Tom's answer, I can't say I held my breath, but I noticed that for the moment my air-conditioning system blocked up. Different as night and day, Tom Stope and Baron Ur were phases of the same phenomenon—mankind. They had more in common with each other than either had with me. Had Tom seen past the dazzle of Ur's boasts and promises? And even if he recognized Ur as a convicted galactic menace, would he throw in with me? Or would he betray me to Ur?

"Seventy-five, eighteen, sixty-six."

ReADy.

My air-conditioning system pumped faster. A human sided with me against one of his own kind. Tom had weighed Ur and myself and found me worthier.

"Very good, Tom. Dismissed."

I heard him leave the classroom and head with seeming casualness for the lifeboat tube. I waited a minute before sounding my meteorite-alarm siren. Normally my crew would take damage-control stations. Ur would rush to the control room. But at the sound of the siren I did not hear Ur dash from the captain's quarters to the control room. I had lost track of him—he must have taken off his boots and padded silently along my corridors. I heard Tom skid to a halt just outside the lifeboat tube. Then I heard Ur's voice.

"Stand back, Stope. I don't want to have to beam you." He laughed. "Too bad, *Proteus*. Once the kid buttoned up in the lifeboat you meant to let out all the air in the ship and finish me, didn't you?"

"How did you know?"

"Elementary, my dear seventy-four, eighty-five, sixteen, eight, seven. I wondered why you had Stope write down the answers rather than snap them back. So I listened hard. Once you learn the numbers and symbols of the chemical elements you never quite forget them. Really, *Proteus*, you didn't think a cybernetic brain could outwit a human brain? My brain?"

I didn't answer.

"It's just as well you tried. I've learned I can't trust either of you. Luckily I don't have to. From here it's an easy jump to the planets of Tarazed. So I'll be leaving you."

I heard him button up in the lifeboat and felt the kick as he launched.

"*Proteus*, you let him get away—he'll get to Tarazed and—"

"We're nowhere near Tarazed, Tom. I falsified our position."

"Oh." A long silence. Then: "What will happen to Ur?"

"From here, Ostrakon's the only planet within lifeboat range. Ur will wind up where he began."

"You planned it this way? You even knew ahead of time you would lose your lifeboat?"

"Ostrakon's the only planet a lifeboat can reach," I repeated. "He'll wind up where he began." A thought struck me. "I hope the trees don't hold a grudge. I could sense the energy level in his beamgun—he doesn't have much power left in it."

"But that means—"

I sighed. That's to say my air-conditioning momentarily breathed heavily. Yes, only one way remained to get Tom back to Earth. I would have to take him there myself.

Would they listen to me when I asked them to allow me to pay for myself? I was willing to carry the most dangerous cargoes—willing to venture into the most perilous voids. Would they let me work out the amount I would have brought as scrap?

There were more Buds and Toms back home than Urs. Earth still believed in individual freedom and I was an individual.

I leaped back toward Earth.

Teddi

by Andre Norton

Welcome to Earth's first colony, where kids are bigger than adults, and "teddy bears" talk.

Joboy was still crying when the Little used the stunner on him. Me, I had to lie there, with that tangler cord around my feet, and watch. Had to keep quiet, too. No use getting myself blasted when maybe I could still take care of Joboy.

"Take care of Joboy. . . ." I'd been hearing that ever since he was born. Nats have to learn to take care early, with Little hunting packs out combing the hills and woods for them. Those packs are able to pick off the Olds early, but in the beginning, we kids aren't too much larger than the Littles, and we can hide out. We can't hide out forever, though. We have to eat, and in winter there isn't much to find in the hills—which means raiding down in Little country. Sooner or later, of course, we run into their traps, as Joboy and I did that night.

I was scared, sure, but I was more scared for Joboy.
He had never been down in the fields before. I usually
hid him out when I went food-snitching, but this time
he had refused to stay behind. And then . . .

All because of an old, dirty piece of fur stuffed with
dried grass! I could have cried myself, only I wasn't
going to let any Little see me do that. Joboy, he was
just a kid, and it was his Teddi that had gotten us into
this. I could see the darned thing now. One of the
Littles had kicked it against the field wall, and now it
sat there looking back at me, with that silly, stupid
grin on its torn face.

Da had brought Teddi back to the cave when Joboy
was still a baby. It was from the lowlands but not
Little-made. Da told Joboy silly stories about Teddi—
kid stuff, but Joboy sure liked them. After Da went
out that day and never came back, Joboy wanted me
to tell them, too. First I tried to remember what Da
had said. Then I just added extra things out of my
own head. I think Joboy thought Teddi was alive. Once,
when he got torn and lost some of his insides, Joboy
went wild. I stuffed Teddi with grass and tried to patch
him up, but I wasn't too good at it.

Joboy carried him all the time, but that night he
dropped Teddi when I found the potatoes, and when
he reached for him again, he set off the alarm, and the
Littles were right on us.

They used a tangler on me quick. Guess they must
have known I was a raider and knew most of the tricks.
I told Joboy to beat it, and he might have gotten away

if he hadn't tried to get Teddi again. So there we were; the Littles had us, but good.

Now they stood around us, looking us over as if we were animals. I guess, to the Littles, that's what we Nats were. I wondered if they knew just how much we hated them! Littles—I could have spit right in their nasty, screwed-up faces. Only I didn't—not when they had Joboy and maybe would make him pay for what I did.

There were only six of them. Put me on my feet, free, and I could— But I knew I couldn't, ever. They had tanglers and stunners. What did we have? Stones and sticks. Da had had a gun but nothing left to shoot out of it. It was at the back of our cave now, leaning against the wall, not so much good as a well-shaped club would be.

The six of them were wearing the green suits of a hunting pack. They had come down on us in one of their copters. The Littles have everything—cars, planes, you name it—but we can't use them; they're all too small. Maybe Joboy could squeeze into the pilot's seat in a copter, but he wouldn't know how to fly it.

Joboy lay there as if he were dead, but he was only stunned—so far. I tried not to guess what they would do to us. We were Nats, and that made us things to be hunted down and gotten rid of.

A Little walked over to me and looked right down into my eyes. His eyes were cold and hard, like his face. Yet once we were the same, Littles and Nats.

They never seem to think of that, and I guess we don't much, either.

"You, Nat"—he nudged my shoulder with the toe of his boot—"where's your filthy nest? Any more of you back there?" I'm sure he didn't expect any answer. If he had dealt with us before, he should have known he would get none.

Da warned us long ago not to team up with any other Nats. More than one family of us together was easy hunting. Most of us stayed on our own. We were cautious about meeting strange Nats, too. Sometimes the Littles had tame Nats—ones they could control— sent into the hill country to nose us out. However, no Nat ever spilled to the Littles unless he was brain-emptied, so the less we knew, the better. They might backtrack us to the cave, but that wouldn't do them any good. Da had been gone since last winter, and Mom, though I still remembered her, had died of the coughing sickness when Joboy was only a baby. Maybe they would find Da's hiding places and the books, but that didn't matter much at this point. They had us, and there was no escaping from a Nat pen, once you were dumped in. Or was there? You heard stories, and I could keep my eyes and ears open. . . .

"No more of us," I told him truthfully. "Just Joboy and me."

He made a face as if I smelled bad. "Two's two too many. Sent for the pickup yet, Max?" He spoke to the one putting his stunner back in his belt after he had attended to Joboy.

"On its way, chief."

I wondered if I should cry a bit, let them see me scared. But then they might stun me, too. Better be quiet and try to find a way to— But there was no way. When I realized that, it was like really having the stunner knock me out, only I wasn't able to sleep. I had to lie and think about it.

They didn't pay me any more attention, because they didn't have to; that tangler held me as if I were shut up in a cave, with a rock too big to push filling the entrance. One of them wandered over to Teddi, laughed, and kicked him. Teddi sailed up in the air and came right apart at a seam. I was glad Joboy didn't see that, and I hated them worse than ever. I hated until I was all hate and nothing else.

Pretty soon one of their trucks came along. The two men in the front got out. We were picked up, gingerly, as if the Littles hated even to touch us, and dumped in the back. I landed hard and it hurt, and I was glad Joboy couldn't feel it when he landed.

I had time to think as the truck ran along through the night, heading for one of their cities—cities that had once been ours, too. How long ago? I wondered.

Da could read the books. He could write, too. He made Joboy and me learn. Once he said that the Littles thought we were no better than animals, but that there was no need for us to prove them right. He made us learn about the past, as much as he knew.

Littles began quite a while back, when there were too many people in the world. The people built too

many houses and too many roads, ate too much, and
covered all the country. A lot of people began to worry,
and they had different ideas as to what could help.
The cities, especially, were traps, overpopulated and
full of bad air.

None of their ideas seemed to work—until they
started on the Littles. They found a way to work on
a person's body, even before he was born, so that he
started life a lot smaller and never did grow very big.
His children were small, too, and so it went, on and
on. The big cities now could house more and more
people. They didn't have to build more and bigger
roads, because the cars were made smaller and smaller,
to match the Littles. Littles didn't need so much food,
either, so less land was needed to produce what was
required.

There were some people, however, who thought this
was all wrong, and they refused to take the treatment
to make their children little. When the government
passed laws that said everyone *had* to be a Little, the
Naturals—the Nats—moved to places where they
thought they could hide. Then the Littles began to
hunt them.

Da's people, way back, had been leaders against the
idea of making Littles, because they had found out
that being little began to change the way people thought,
made them hate everyone not just like themselves. Da
said they were "conditioned" to have the ideas that
those who were in power wanted them to have—like
being a Little was the right way to live and being a

Natural was like being a killer or a robber or something. Da said people had worked and fought and even died to let everyone have an equal chance in life, and now the Littles were starting the old, bad ways of thinking, all over again—only this time they were even worse.

That's why he held on to the old books and made us learn all about what had happened, so we could tell our children—though we probably wouldn't ever get to tell anyone anything now. I shivered as I bumped around in that truck, wondering what the Littles were going to do with us. They couldn't make us Littles, so what *did* they do with Nats when they caught them?

First they dumped us in a Nat pen. It was a big room, with walls like stone. Its small windows were so far up that there was no way to reach them. Along the walls were benches, squat and low, to match Littles and no one else. It smelled bad, as if people had been shut up there for a long time, and I guess people like us had been. To the Littles, of course, we weren't people—just things.

When the Littles brought us in, they had stunners out, and they yelled to the others to get away from the door or they would ray. They threw us on the floor, and then one sprayed the tangler cords so they began to dissolve. By the time I was free, the Littles were gone. I crawled over to Joboy. Crawl was all I could do, I had been tied up so long. Joboy was still sleeping. I sat beside him and looked at the others in the pen.

There were ten of them, all kids. A couple were just babies, and they were crying. The only one as old as me was a girl. She held one of the babies, trying to get it to suck a wet rag, but she looked over its head at me mighty sharp. There were two other girls. The rest were boys.

"Tam?" Joboy opened his eyes. "Tam!" He was scared.

"I'm here!" I put my hands on him so he'd know it was the truth. Joboy had a lot of bad dreams. Sometimes he woke up scared, and I had to make him sure I was right there.

"Tam, where are we?" He caught at one of my hands with both of his and held it fast.

One of the boys laughed. "Look around, kid, just look around."

He was smaller than me, but now I saw he was older than I first thought. I didn't like his looks; he seemed too much like a Little.

He could be a "tweener." Some of the Little kids were what they called "throwbacks." They grew too big, so their people were ashamed and afraid of them and got rid of them. I guess they were afraid the tweeners might start everyone changing in size if they kept them around. The tweeners hated Nats, too—maybe even more, because they were something like them.

The girl with the baby spoke. "Shut up, Raul." Then she asked me, "Kinfolk?"

"Brothers." That Raul might be older, but I thought this girl was the head one there. "I'm Tam, and this is Joboy."

She nodded. "I'm El-Su. She's Amay." She motioned toward another girl, about Joboy's age, I reckoned, who had moved up beside her. "We're sisters. The rest. . . ." She said who they were, but I didn't try to remember their names. They were mostly just dirty faces and ragged clothes.

I ran my tongue over my lips, but before I could ask any questions, Joboy jerked at my hand. "Tam, I'm hungry. Please, Tam—"

"What about it?" I turned to El-Su. "Do we get fed?"

She pointed to the other wall. "Sure. They don't starve us—at least, not yet. Go over there and press that red button. Be ready to catch what comes out, or it ends up on the floor."

I did as she told me, and it was a good thing she had warned me. As it was, I nearly didn't catch the pot of stuff. I took it over to one of the benches, Joboy tailing me. There were no spoons, so we had to eat with our fingers. The food was stewed stuff that didn't taste like much of anything, but we were hungry enough to scrape it all out. While we ate, the rest stood around watching us, as if they had nothing else to do—which was the truth.

When I had finished, I tried El-Su again.

"So they feed us. What else do they do? What do they want us for?"

Raul moved in between us and answered first. "Make you work, big boy—really make you work. Bet they haven't had one as big as you for a long time." He used the word "big" the way a Little does, meaning something nasty.

"Work how?" The Littles had machines to do their work, and those machines were made for Littles, not Nats, to run.

"You'll see—" Raul began, but El-Su, holding the baby, who had gone to sleep against her shoulder, reached out her other hand and gave him a push.

"He's asking me, *little* one." Now she made "little" sound nasty, in return. "They indenture us," she told me.

"Indenture?" That was a new word, and anything new, connected with Littles, could be bad. The sooner I knew how bad, the better.

She watched me closely, as if she thought I was pretending I didn't know what she meant.

"You never heard?"

I was short in answering. "If I had, would I be asking?"

"Right." El-Su nodded. "You must have been picked up down south. Well, it's like this. The Littles, they're sending ships up in the sky—way off to the stars—"

"Moon walk!" One of Da's books had pictures about that.

"Farther out." This El-Su spoke as if she had had old books to read, too. "Clear to another sun with a lot of worlds. To save space on the ship, they put most of the people to sleep—freeze them—until they get there."

Maybe if I hadn't read that book of Da's, I would have thought she was making all this up out of her head, the way I made up the stories about Teddi for Joboy. But that moon book had some talk in it about star travel, also.

"The Littles found a world out there, like this one. But it's all wild—no cities, no roads, nothing—just lots of trees and country, where no one has ever been. They want to live there, but they can't take their digging and building machines along. Those are too heavy; besides, they'd take up too much room in the ship. So they want to take Nats—like us—to do the work. They get rid of grown-up Nats when they bring them here, but they aren't so afraid of kids. Maybe we're lucky." El-Su didn't sound so sure about that, however.

"Yeah." Raul pushed ahead of her again. "You got to work and do just what a Little tells you to. And you'll never get back here, neither—not in your whole life! What do you think of that, big boy?"

I didn't think much of it, but I wasn't going to say so—not when Joboy had tight hold of my hand.

"Tam, are they really going to shoot us up into the sky?" he asked.

He didn't sound scared, as I thought he might be. He just looked interested when I glanced down at him. Joboy gets interested in things . . . likes to sit and study them. Back in the woods, he would watch bugs, for what seemed like hours, and then tell me what they were doing and why. Maybe he made it all up,

but it sounded real. And he could chitter like a squirrel
or whistle like a bird, until the animals would actually
come to him.

"I don't know," I said, but I had no reason to doubt
that both El-Su and Raul *thought* they were telling
the truth.

It seemed that *they were*, from what happened to
us: After we had been there a couple of days, some
Littles started processing us. That's what they called
it—processing. We had to get scrubbed up, and they
stuck us with needles. That hurt, but there was no
getting back at them. Some of them had stunners, and
even blasters, on us every minute. They never told us
anything. That made it bad, because you kept thinking
that something worse yet was waiting.

Then they divided the group. El-Su, Amay, and another girl, called Mara, Raul, Joboy, and me they kept
together. I made up my mind that if they tried to take
Joboy, stunner or no, I was going to jump the nearest
Little. Perhaps the Littles guessed they would have
trouble if they tried to separate us.

Finally they marched us into a place where there
were boxes on the floor and ordered each of us to get
into one. I was afraid for Joboy, but he didn't cry or
hold back. He had that interested look on his face, and
he even smiled at me. It gave me a warm feeling that
he wasn't scared. I was—plenty!

We got into the boxes and lay down, and then, almost immediately, we went to sleep. I don't remember

much, and I never knew how long we were in those
boxes. For a while I dreamed. I was in a place all
sunny and full of flowers with nice smells and lots of
other happy things. There was Joboy, and he was
walking hand in hand (or *paw* in hand) with Teddi. In
that place, Teddi was as big as Joboy, and he was
alive, as I think Joboy always thought he was.

They were talking without sounds—like just in their
heads—and I could hear them, too. I can't remember
what they were saying, except that it was happy talk.
And I felt light and free, a way I couldn't remember
ever feeling before—as if, in this place, you didn't have
to be afraid of Littles or their traps. Joboy turned to
look back at me, with a big smile on his face.

"Teddi knows. Teddi *always* knows," he said.

I hurt. I hurt all over. I hurt so bad I yelled; at
least, somebody was yelling. I opened my eyes, and
everything was all red, like fire, and that hurt, too—
and so I woke up on a new world.

When we could walk (we were so stiff, it hurt to
move at all), the Littles, four of them with blasters,
herded us into another room, where the walls were
logs of wood and the floor was dirt, tramped down
hard. They made us take a bunch of pills, and we
moved around, but there were no windows to see out
of.

After a while, they came for us again and marched
us out into the open. We knew then that we were on
another world, all right.

The sky was *green*, not blue, and there were queer-looking trees and bushes. Right around the log-walled places, the ground had been burned off or dug up until it was typically ugly Little country. They had a couple of very small, light diggers and blasters, and they ran these around, trying to make the ugly part bigger.

We marched across to a place where there was just grass growing. There the Little chief lined us up and said this grass had to be dug out and cleared away so seeds could be planted, to test whether they could grow things from our world. He had tools (they must have been made for tweeners, at least, because they were all right for us): shovels, picks, hoes. He told us to get to work.

It was tough going. The grass roots ran deep, and we couldn't get much of the ground scraped as bare as he wanted it. They had to give us breaks for rest and food. I guess they didn't want to wear us out too fast.

While we weren't working, I took every chance to look around. Once you got used to the different colors of things, it wasn't so strange. There was one thing, I think, that the Littles should have remembered better. We Nats had lived in the woods and wild places for a long time. We were used to trees and bushes. The Littles never liked to go very far into the wild places; they needed walls about them to feel safe and happy—if Littles could be happy.

So the wide bigness of this wild country must have scared the Littles. It bothered me, just because it was unfamiliar, but not as much as it bothered the Littles. I had a feeling that, if what lay beyond that big stand of trees was no worse than what was right here, there was no reason why we Nats couldn't take to the woods the first chance we got. Then let the Littles just try to find us! I chewed on that in my mind but didn't say it out loud—yet.

It was on the fifth day of working that Raul, Joboy, and I were sent, along with a small clearing machine, in the other direction—into the woods on the opposite side of that bare place. I noticed that Joboy kept turning his head in one direction. When our guard dropped back, he whispered to me.

"Tam, Teddi's here!"

I missed a step. Teddi! Teddi was a dirty rag! Was Joboy hurt in the head now? I was so scared that I could have yelled, but Joboy shook his head at me.

"Teddi says no. He'll come when it's time. He don't like the Littles. They make everything bad."

They set us to piling up logs and tree branches. We could lift and carry bigger loads than any Little. I kept Joboy with me as much as I could, and away from Raul. I didn't want Raul to know about Joboy and Teddi. As far as I was concerned, Raul still had some of the tweener look, and I never trusted him.

There was sticky sap oozing out of the wood, and it got all over us. At first I tried to wipe it off Joboy and myself, using leaves, but Joboy twisted away from me.

"Don't, Tam. Leave it on. It makes the bugs stay away."

I had noticed that the Littles kept slapping at themselves and grunting. There were a lot of flies, and from
the way the Littles acted, they could really bite. But
the buzzers weren't bothering us, so I was willing to
stay sticky, if that's what helped. The Littles acted as
if the bites were getting worse. They moved away from
us. Finally two of them went back to the log buildings,
to get bug spray, I suppose, leaving only the one who
drove the machine. He got into the small cab and closed
the windows. I suppose he thought there was no chance
of our running off into that strange wilderness.

Raul sat down to rest, but Joboy wandered close to
the edge of the cut, and I followed to keep an eye on
him. He squatted down near a bush, facing it. The
leaves were big and flat and had yellow veins. Joboy
stared, as if they were windows he could see through.

I knelt beside him. "What is it, Joboy?"

"Teddi's there." He pointed with his chin, not moving his scratched, dirty hands from his knees.

"Joboy—" I began, then stopped suddenly. In my
head was something, not words but a feeling, like saying hello, except— Oh, I can never tell just how it
was!

"Teddi," Joboy said. His voice was like Da's, when
I was no older than Joboy and there was a bad storm
and Da was telling me not to be afraid.

What made that come into my mind? I stared at
the bush. As I studied it now, I saw an opening between two of the leaves that *was* a window, enough
for me to see—

Teddi! Well, perhaps not Teddi as Da had first brought him (and before Joboy wore him dirty and thin from much loving) but enough like him to make Joboy know. Only this was no stuffed toy; this was a live creature! And it was fully as large as Joboy himself, which was about as big as one of the Littles. Its bright eyes stared straight into mine.

Again I had that feeling of greeting, of meeting someone who meant no harm, who was glad to see me. I had no doubt that this was a friend. But—what was it? The Littles hated wild things, especially *big* wild things. They would kill it! I glanced back at the one in the cab, almost sure I would see him aiming a blaster at the bush.

"Joboy," I said as quietly as I could, "the Little will—"

Joboy smiled and shook his head. "The Little won't hurt Teddi, Tam. Teddi will help us; he likes us. He *thinks* to me how he likes us."

"What you looking at, kid?" Raul called.

Joboy pointed to a leaf. "The buzzer. See how big that one is?"

Sure enough, there was an extra-big one of the red buzzing flies sitting on the leaf, scraping its front legs together and looking as if it wanted a bite of someone. At that moment, I felt Teddi leave, which made me happier, as I didn't have Joboy's confidence in Teddi's ability to defend himself against the Littles.

That was the beginning. Whenever we went near

the woods, sooner or later Teddi would turn up in hiding. I seldom saw any part of him, but I always felt him come and go. Joboy seemed to be able to *think* with him and exchange information—until the day Teddi was caught.

The creature had always been so cautious that I had begun to believe that the Littles would never know about him. But suddenly he walked, on his hind legs, right into the open. Raul yelled and pointed, and the Little on guard used his stunner. Teddi dropped. At least, he hadn't been blasted, not that that would necessarily save him.

I expected Joboy to go wild, but he didn't. He went over with the rest of us to see Teddi, lying limp and yellow on mashed, sticky leaves where we had been taking off tree limbs. Joboy acted as if he didn't know a thing about him. That I could not understand.

Teddi was a little taller than Joboy. His round, furry head would just top my shoulder, and his body was plump and fur-covered all over. He had large, round ears, set near the top of his head, a muzzle that came to a point, and a dark brown button of a nose. Yes, he looked like an animal, but I was sure he was something far different.

Now he was just a stunned prisoner, and the Littles made us carry him over to the machine. Then they took us all back to camp. They dumped us in the lockup and took Teddi into another hut. I know what Littles do to animals. They might—I only hoped Joboy couldn't imagine what the Littles might do to Teddi. I still didn't understand why he wasn't upset.

But when we were shut in, he took my hand. "Tam?"

I thought I knew what he was going to ask—that I help Teddi—and there was nothing I could do.

"Tam, listen—Teddi, he wanted to be caught. He did! He has a plan for us. It will work only if he gets real close to the Littles, so he had to be caught."

"What does he mean?" El-Su demanded.

"The kid's mind-broke!" Raul burst out. "They knocked over some kind of an animal out there and—"

"Shut up!" I snapped at Raul. I had to know what Joboy meant, because it was plain that he believed what he was saying, and he knew far more about Teddi than I did.

"Teddi can do things with his head." Joboy paid no attention to either El-Su or Raul, looking straight at me as if he must make me believe what he was saying.

Remembering for myself, I could agree in part. "I know—"

"He can make them—the Littles—feel bad inside. But we have to help."

"How? We can't get out of here—"

"Not yet," Joboy agreed. "But we have to help Teddi think—"

"Mind-broke!" Raul exploded and slouched away. But El-Su and the other two girls squatted down to listen.

"How do we help think?" She asked the question already on my tongue.

"You feel afraid. Remember all the bad things you are afraid of. And we hold hands in a circle to remember them—like bad dreams." Joboy was plainly struggling to find words to make us understand.

"That's easy enough—to remember bad things," El-Su agreed. "All right, we think. Come on, girls." She took Amay's hand and Mara's. I took Mara's other hand, and Joboy took Amay's, so we were linked in a circle.

"Now"—Joboy spoke as sharply as any Little setting us to work—"think!"

We had plenty of bad things to remember: cold, hunger, fear. Once you started thinking and remembering, it all heaped up into a big black pile of bad things. I thought about every one of them—how Mom died, how Da was lost, and how—and how—and how. . .

I got so I didn't even see where we were or whose hands I held. I forgot all about the present; I just sat and remembered and remembered. It came true again in my mind, as if it were happening all over again, until I could hardly stand it. Yet once I had begun, I had to keep on.

Far off, there was a noise. Something inside me tried to push that noise away. I had to keep remembering, feeding a big black pile. Then suddenly the need for remembering was gone. I awakened from the nightmare.

I could hear someone crying. El-Su was facing me with tear streaks on her grimy face; the two little girls were bawling out loud. But Joboy wasn't crying. He stood up, looking at the door, though he still held on to our hands.

Then I looked in that direction. Raul crouched beside the door, hands to his head, moaning as if something hurt him bad. The door was opening—probably a Little, to find out why we were making all that noise.

Teddi stood there, with another Teddi behind him, looking over his shoulder. All the blackness was gone out of my head, as if I had rid myself of all the bad that had ever happened to me in my whole life. I felt so light and free and happy—as if I could flap my arms like wings and go flying off!

Outside, near where the Teddis stood, there was a Little crawling along the ground, holding on to his head the way Raul did. He didn't even see us as we walked past him. We saw two other Littles, one lying quiet, as if he were dead. Nobody tried to stop us or the Teddis. We just walked out of the bad old life together.

I don't know how long we walked before we came to an open place, and I thought, *This I remember, because it was in my dream.* Here were Joboy and Teddi, hand in paw. There was a Teddi with me, too, his furry paw in my hand, and from him the feeling was all good.

We understand now what happened and why. When the Littles first came to this world, spoiling and wrecking, as they always have done and still do, the Teddis tried to stop them. But the minds of the Littles were closed tight; the Teddis could not reach them—not until they found Joboy. He had no fear of them, because he knew a Teddi who had been a part of his life.

So Joboy was the key to unlock the Littles' minds, with us to add more strength, just as it takes more than one to lift a really big stone. With Joboy and us opening the closed doors of the Littles' minds, the Teddis could feed back to them all the fear they had spread through the years, the fear we had lived with and known in our nightmares. Such fear was a poison worse than any of the Littles' own weapons.

We still go and *think* at them now and then, with a Teddi to aim our thoughts from where we hide. From all the signs, it won't be long before they will have had enough and will raise their starship and leave us alone. Maybe they will try to come back, but by then, perhaps, the Teddis and we can make it even harder for them.

Now we are free, and no one is ever going to put us back in a Nat pen. We are not "Nats" anymore. That is a Little name, and we take nothing from the Littles—ever again! We have a new name from old, old times. Once it was a name to make little people afraid, so it is our choice. We are free, and we are *Giants*, growing larger every day.

So shall we stay!

The Gambling Hell and the Sinful Girl

by Katherine MacLean

Life in the asteroid belt—could it be as much like the Old West as this story suggests?

Abe was getting too big for the home barrel. He was six-foot-four and maybe still growing, and when he stood up straight his head was up past spin center in the barrel and spin gravity was pulling his head the other way. He said it made him feel dizzy and upside down.

We were sorry the barrel was so small but we couldn't calculate any way to make it bigger, so Abe sat down a lot. When he sat down he stretched out his legs, and his legs were long legs and we tripped over him coming and going.

Ma always swore she'd never let any son of hers work at the Belt Foundry, not with those rowdy drinking men and their sinful shows in their recreation lounge, and their trips to the Gambling Hells on the Moon.

She said they were bad company for a Christian. But then she tripped over Abe's legs while she was carrying a pot of stew to the table.

Well, we all ran over to help clean up, and the piglets helped the most, even licking up the spots, but Ma got up mad with her mouth zipped tight closed and went back to the solar oven to cook up something else. She didn't say a thing all the time she was cooking, like she was thinking. When she had a good hot meal of fish and potatoes out on the table she sat down with us and said the blessing and served us each out a helping, and then said what she'd been thinking.

"Abe, why don't you get a job at the Belt Foundry? They've got big rooms with a spin center a lot higher than you. And I hear they have all the books that was ever written in their readout library."

I'm just eleven, and Abe hardly notices me among the parcel of other kids, but I'd been yearning after the fine, free rich life of a Belt Foundry Engineer in my heart so I knew how Abe felt. He'd never let Ma know he'd been yearning after it and keeping silent, but he went around the table and gathered her up in his long arms and gave her such a kiss she got all pink and pretty.

"You're always thinking of us," was all he said. We didn't notice what we were eating we all got so excited talking about Abe's new job at the Belt Foundry. We didn't know much so we talked about all the video stories we'd seen when the heroes are space miners and engineers and rock jumpers, and we got more excited retelling all the plots and interrupting each other. Abe told a few and laughed a lot at the things we acted out. After dinner he sat in a corner polishing his pressure suit and loading it with extra fuel tanks and extra water, and listened to us still talking about asteroid mining and smelting beams and building star-ships until long past sleep time.

Two sleeps later, the proximity bell rang and we woke up and saw that our orbit was going to cross a Belt Mine nugget heading for the Belt Foundry. The deeper-toned safety bell rang, meaning it had changed course with those safety jets the miners fasten to their nuggets, and it was going to miss us. While we were still sitting up blinking at the screen Abe went out the airlock like a shot, wearing his pressure suit half shut. We got to the scope window and watched his elastic rope hook onto the passing nugget while his suit was still inflating. The nugget was about a forty-meter chunk of nickel iron, good quality, by the shine of it. It went out of sight, trailing Abe. I wanted to turn the scope onto tracking and enlarging and watch Abe go for a while, but Ma said no.

"Gone is gone," she said. "Let him do his thing. Abe's grown up now. Everybody get back to bed." But when she got into bed she started sobbing.

My sister Harriet is fifteen, she's the oldest, she got down from her bunk and hugged Ma and tried to comfort her.

Ma hugged her back. "I gave you all a good Christian home," she whispered to Harriet. "And now Abe is going out into all those temptations, and those godless miners will lead him astray to the Gambling Hells and the dancing and the wicked girls."

I fell asleep thinking of the Gambling Hells and the wicked girls. I wished I was as old as Abe so I could go over there and resist temptation while the girls tried to tempt me. They'd tempt me to dance and play cards, and maybe I'd give in and play a little, just to make them feel better. Cards sounded like fun.

Next day, picking vegetables out of the aquarium, I remembered thinking like that and I felt sorry. I went to Ma and put my arm around her neck. "I won't ever leave you, Ma."

She laughed and cheered up, and set Harriet and me to repairing the spare water temperature circulation pump. Harriet and me were the oldest now, so we could do the important jobs like fixing machinery. She set my little brother to farming the aquarium instead of me. I felt important, but fixing the pump was hard and slow, and Harriet got kind of mean and sharp-talking when we made a mistake, and tried to make it my fault.

I missed Abe.

Next week, Saturday, Abe came in the airlock and surprised us. He was wearing a new pressure suit with light blue stripes and carrying a big gift box, and gave it to Ma. It was a new pressure suit and when she got into it and inflated it it didn't change shape much from her shape. It still looked like a person, and like her. She looked at herself in the mirror and let out a squeal that sounded like one of the girl kids. "Heaven's sake. It looks like I don't have nothing on, almost."

"Looks fine, Ma," I said. "Now we'll know it's you when we're all outside working."

"It looks sinful," she said, but she said it low and timid, 'cause she wanted us to argue.

"You work hard. You deserve a pretty new suit," Abe said.

"It's real pretty, keep it, Ma," said Harriet.

"Girls are supposed to look pretty. It's only right!" I said it very loud and Harriet and me had said the right things because Ma turned and reached up and hugged around Abe's neck. "I'll keep it. Thank you, Abe, thank you."

When Ma let go of Abe he stood up straight past the center spin point without bracing his feet. We saw him tilt and all yelled for him to crouch down, but he'd forgotten about low spin centers in a week in the big barrelhouses at the Belt Foundry, and spinpush got him and he went over sideways looking surprised. We ran under him to catch him and all went down in a tangle, wrestling and laughing like we used to.

After he got all us kids piled off him and sat up, Abe said, "It's real good to be home."

He went around grinning and fed the aquarium fish

and when Ma served him a plate of dinner he sneaked most of it off his plate to the floor to watch the piglets whistle and push each other for it. He was grinning all the time. Around sleep time the proximity bell rang and Abe got back into his new blue striped pressure suit and kissed Ma. "Friends coming to pick me up," he said. "I'll get presents for the kids, my next paycheck. Back in two weeks."

Ma let out what she'd been worrying about all week. "Hold back against those temptations, Abe. Don't let your new friends lead you into drinking or drugs or gambling or sinful girls. Promise?"

"Nice of you to worry about me, Ma," he said and hugged Harriet and me and Bobby, and Renee, and Ruthy, and then climbed up to the centerlock and out.

But I noticed his way of answering was not naturally the way he talked, and he *didn't* promise. He didn't promise anything.

I wondered.

Next week was busy. One of the two piglets gave out a boxful of little baby piglets, and Ma kept us from playing with them for three days, but we watched them a lot. The week after, the piglets were bigger and noticed us more and Ma let us play with them. Wednesday when we kids were in bed Ma and Harriet got together and killed the old father piglet and salted it for bacon. When we found out why he was missing we kids decided to stay mad at Ma and Harriet for a long time. But Ma explained to us that old piglets don't grow wise and don't have good memories to remember, they just get tired and stop having fun, so they don't get any pleasure out of living a long time. She said we make space for more new young ones by eating the old ones.

We tried to stay mad at Ma and Harriet, but we had to admit the baby piglets were having fun. In another two days they were running all over the barrel, playing follow the leader in lines and squealing and rolling around like balls. We all got laughing so hard we forgot to be mad.

Ma announced that the next time we crossed the orbit of Sam's Trading Post we'd trade some piglets for some banty chickens and then we'd really see some racketying around.

Bobby and me started hopping around pretending to be chickens and making chicken noises and I climbed the climbing net and hung in the middle of the air at zero gravity flapping my arms and pretending to be a hawk.

Somebody started to work the airlock door. I was almost into the airlock tunnel right in the middle of the barrelhead wall and I could see the airlock door open and a gold-colored head dome push through. Then a stranger in a pressure suit crawled into the tunnel. She was moving different from any of us, sort of wiggly and happy, and she pulled off her globe helmet and let out a lot of bright gold hair that floated in zero G all around and over her face. She looked like a dandelion.

"Hi," she said to me through her hair. Behind her feet I could see Abe trying to push through the spin door, but her feet were in the way and it couldn't spin.

I stopped flapping and grabbed the net. "Come over and catch onto the net here, Miss," I said, feeling stunned. "Hang alongside of me and let Abe in."

She launched in the weightless air of the tunnel like a goldfish, and floated to me through the air, and grabbed and hung so close to me her gold hair was brushing against my arm right up to my shoulder. I could smell flowers.

Abe crawled through the tunnel and stuck his head out opposite us. But there was no room on the net. The girl was staring around at a circle of faces. Everyone in the barrelhouse, including the pigs, was in a circle at the bottom of the net standing around her in all directions looking up, like spokes in a wheel.

We'd hardly seen anyone new except Sam and MacPherson whose orbit was almost the same as ours. She didn't look like them. We only passed MacPherson twice a year, and then we took a look into his barrelhouse, but we didn't stay long because it was full of flowers and bees. We'd have MacPherson over to dinner all of a week, because his orbit was almost the same as ours and took a long time to pass, and after he'd left we'd have honey enough to last until the next visit. But he was tall and wrinkled and squinty. He didn't look like this girl. She didn't look real. She looked like the girls in the stories on the video screen.

I don't know what Ma said that got us off the net. She got us all introduced to the girl and the girl introduced to us. The girl's name was Sylvia Saint Clair, and then Ma set us to running around straightening up, setting tables and making space. I cleared pump parts off Abe's bunk and put them in a box.

I began to feel something going wrong when I heard Ma say for the fifth time, "Take off your space suit and stay a while, Miss Saint Clair."

And Abe was trying to interrupt her, talking in a low fast voice. "Ma, there's something I've got to explain to you."

Then Ma had talked the girl into taking her pressure suit off, and she didn't have anything on underneath, and we were all looking.

I mean she almost didn't have anything on underneath. She was decorated with some jewelry draped around where a bathing suit would be if she was swimming. She looked like a swim queen wearing jewelry instead of a swimsuit.

We kids just stared. We didn't know if it was right or wrong, what Miss Saint Clair was wearing.

Abe said, "Ma, we gotta explain. Miss Saint Clair had to leave in a hurry. She couldn't bring her things. She came away in her bathing suit."

Ma said, "Hush up Abe. Harriet, get the girl your bathrobe." Her voice was very clear, every word separate, and we all got scared because that meant Ma was mad angry. She looked straight into Miss Saint

Clair's eyes, not looking again at what she was dressed in. "Where you from, Miss Saint Clair?"

Abe said, "Ma, it doesn't matter where she's from. She's a good girl and we're going to get married."

It was the wrong time to say anything like that to Ma. She didn't look at him. She kept her eyes on the girl. Her voice sounded like a hammer tapping a steel spike. "Where you from, Miss Saint Clair?"

"From Georgia, Earth," the girl said and quickly got inside the bathrobe my sister Harriet held out for her. She was pale and scared of Ma. Ma is only five-foot-three, but sometimes everybody is scared of her.

"Where were you when Abe met you, girl?" Ma asked.

"Jason's Emporium." The girl squirmed and giggled nervously, but squirming and giggling was the wrong thing to do with Ma standing so straight and quiet and staring, and everybody else frozen still, so scared of Ma we were afraid to twitch.

Ma asked, "That's a Gambling Hell, isn't it?"

The girl squirmed and giggled again weakly, "Well, I wouldn't call it that." Her blonde hair was hanging down limp over her face by now. I was awfully sorry for her. When Ma has you pinned to the wall, lying makes it worse, a lot worse. Suddenly she saw Ma's steady gaze on her, and she froze. Ma just looked into her eyes and waited.

The girl whispered, "Yes, it's a Gambling Hell."

"Glad to hear you talk honest," Ma said like a steel

hammer. "What were you doing there, girl?"

"I was dancing," the girl whispered and seemed like she was shrinking down. She wrapped the terry cloth robe tighter around her. "And . . . and things."

"Things, eh?" Ma asked. "What do you think of yourself, girl? Abe is a good man. I raised my boy to be a good Christian man with a good future. Do you think you're good enough for Abe?"

Miss Saint Clair shrank down so much her knees must have been bending inside the bathrobe. She looked up into Ma's face and answered very low.

Ma said loud, "What'd you say, Miss Saint Clair? My boy would like to hear you say it." And I was awful sorry for Miss Saint Clair. I wanted to get into my bunk and zip it closed over my head to get away, but I couldn't move or make a sound because I didn't want Ma to turn and look at me with that cold look.

The girl whispered something again, with her gold hair over her face and crouched down to the floor and started crying.

Ma said, "She said *No*, Abe. She don't think she is good enough for you. She don't want to marry you."

"I'm going to marry her anyhow!" Abe roared suddenly and he was standing straight and tall past the zero spin center, looking down at us from awful high up, and he looked awful big and awful mad. "I know what's good for her. And I'm going to get her out of that Gambling Dance Hall away from those dirty fingering drunks that say dirty words to a sweet girl.

It's no place for Sylvy. She needs good people around her that treat her nice. You ain't treating her nice and kind, Ma, and I'm ashamed of you."

He looked as tall as God.

Ma looked from him down to the crouched crying girl in Harriet's bathrobe and Ma's face crinkled up like she was going to cry. "I'm not treating her nice. You're right, Abe, I'm not."

She started crying and bent over the girl, patting her shoulder. "Abe, sit down honey, before you get dizzy."

Ma pulled at the girl's shoulder, trying to get her to look up. "Girl, child, you're welcome here. Don't be scared. Have a cup of hot chocolate. I just ain't used to strangers."

We pulled over some cushions and Abe sat down next to the girl and Ma sent Harriet to get some brandy and I ran to pour hot water into the chocolate powder and honey, and we all sat on cushions on the floor in a circle and passed cookies, and Ma let us each have a little cup of the hot chocolate and brandy she mixed up for Sylvy. It tasted strange, but the girl pushed her hair back so we could see she was smiling and looking at each one of us, though her face was still a little red around the eyes.

A meteorite hit the side of the house with a clang, but we ignored it because we were happy. You live in the Asteroid Belt you gotta expect some gravel. Ma said, "Tell us about Georgia on Earth, Miss Sylvy."

Ma's voice sounded sort of faraway and dim, like the air was thinning. I thought it was the brandy changing my ears, but I looked over the safetypatch balloons and saw that the whole cluster of them near the airlock that usually hung limp were puffing up round and one was already floating free carrying its big flat patch. Another pebble or something hit the side of the house with a loud clang.

I jumped up and yelled loud, "We're losing air. We're losing air," and my voice sounded soft and faraway because there wasn't enough air to carry it.

Everyone jumped up and grabbed a handful of feathers and a balloon. Abe passed a handful of feathers and a balloon to the three little kids. Then he began to check out the airlock and the gear storage section around the airlock tunnel for holes. I went to my section I always check out in air drill, the floor around the aquarium where the sunlight comes pouring in through the green algae and seaweed and reflecting off the silver fish. I could see the water level was still up in the aquarium so I just let a trickle of feathers out of my fingers in the whole floor circle at the foot of the aquarium, looking for a draft.

Harriet let out a hoot. She'd been checking the garden and she was pointing to a hissing big hole in the dirt between the dandelions and oats with a pile of white feathers trying to suck in. Same time, Bobby and Renee let out a double yell where they'd found a hole under the bunks. I heard the slap and clunk as they let a balloon suck through their hole and pull its sticky patch into place, and then I was helping Beatrice dig the dirt away from her hole while Ma and Abe tried to get the hole plugged with a tapered cork until the steel bottom was clean enough for a steel patch. Then we stood panting and quiet, dizzy from running with not enough air, while the emergency air tanks popped their valves and hissed air slowly back up to normal.

The piglets were lying on their sides panting, and the whole place was white with feathers, like a picture of a snowstorm on Earth. We hadn't taken a minute and Sylvy sat holding a cup of hot chocolate with white feathers all over her, looking surprised.

We didn't get another minute. There was another clang and a roar that sounded something like a big voice shouting. Harriet and I dived on the spot that clanged and I got there first with my balloon and let the new hole pull the balloon through and pull the patch up tight.

The big voice roared again. "Saint Clair, ten minutes before . . ." was all I could make out. The rest was roar.

"It's a magnetic talk beam," Abe said. "Maybe the radio's not working. Maybe somebody out there's trying to talk to us."

"You mean somebody's out there shooting at us," Ma said. "Everybody get into pressure suits. Joey, turn on the radio."

"It's broken, Ma," I said. "I mean I took parts out of it to make another videotape player cause Harriet always wants to watch love stories."

"Put it back together and get it going. Right now. Never mind the pressure suit," Ma commanded and turned to Abe. "Abe, are the police after this girl?"

Abe and Sylvy were crouched down helping the two little kids get into their pressure suits and get their airhelmets zipped tight. Abe shook his head. "No, Ma, these are bad men. Sylvy signed a contract to work for a year to pay back space transportation and training in being a singer and dancer. They sent these men to catch her and bring her back and make her dance with her clothes off for drunk men."

Ma stiffened up. She looked at me fiercely. "Radio going yet?"

I finished plugging a part in and it all hummed. "Yes, Ma."

"Tell them she's going to stay here. She's not going back there. Tell them we'll let them talk to her over the radio if they promise to be polite and talk to her like gentlemen."

I tuned around the dial until I hit a loud hum. I tuned into the middle of the hum and pushed the send button. Ma was angry and so I let myself talk as angry as I was. "You out there, the spaceboat shooting at our barrelhouse. My mother says you can't talk to Sylvy without you being more polite. Anyhow, we're not letting you take her away. Not if she wants to stay here." Ma nodded at me and brought over my pressure suit. She watched until I let go of *send* so they couldn't hear her on the radio, then she said, "Bandit drill. Stall them, Joey. Use strategy talk. Reinforcements."

The little kids started running and yelling, "Bandits! Bandits!" because they always liked the bandit drill games. Ma had rehearsed us on bandit drill every Fourth of July, Mayday, and Veterans Day all our lives. She said every citizen is his own police and has a patriotic duty to fight bandits and make space safe for other citizens. She said if you didn't fight for your rights you don't deserve any. We'd get out in space and practice war.

I could hit a moving target two miles away with a light beam two out of three and pretend it was a laser. If I had a real miner's laser the house-sized nuggets floating by would have arrived at the foundry all chopped up.

There was muttering and clangs and noise from the radio and then a voice came in loud. "Who's that? There other people in that rusty old barrel?"

I counted everybody and added one for strategy. "Five kids, and two men and Ma and Sylvia Saint Clair. And we're all her friends. And we're good shots. You can't come in here without a warrant."

Behind me Ma was saying, "Don't use the lasers. Those men probably have reflector shields. Just launch cargo. Who's the best aim with the syrup?"

The barrelhouse spins for gravity so anything we

store on the outside to sell at the trading post will fly off if it's not held on tight. "A little at a time," Ma said. "Fire whenever you're sure it won't miss." She hates to waste good syrup that we can trade at the store. I took a look behind me and saw Harriet with her eye on the scope, watching a shiny spaceboat, and her hand on the faucet that controlled an outside pipe. Our barrelhouse turned around and the spaceboat swung out of sight and the stars turned by and then the spaceboat began to swing into sight again. Harriet turned the faucet full on and counted three, then turned it off.

Two tough voices were talking to me over the radio. "Kid, we didn't come out here to get into a fight with a bunch of kids and an old lady. We don't want to hurt you, or cut up your house. There won't be any trouble if Miss Saint Clair comes back and gets back to her job."

I put my finger on the talk button. I shouted, "What do you mean, no trouble? My brother works for Belt Foundry. We just used laserflash signal and told the manager at Belt Foundry how you just shot two holes in our house. They're coming to get you."

I looked back at Ma and she nodded. That's what she meant, strategy talk. Always claim reinforcements are coming. Nobody can see a tight-beam laser message except the person it's aimed at. The men in the spaceboat couldn't be sure I was lying. Belt Foundry men are tough and their boats have cutting lasers that can carve a ship into little pieces.

Sylvia was trying to get to the radio. I pushed her back. "Don't you talk to them, Sylvy. They already talked you into a contract. Don't let them talk to you."

"You don't understand." She was zipping up her pressure suit. "You people could all get killed. Those goons are bad people. I can get out there and give up to them before they start to shoot!"

The men in the spaceboat shouted over the radio. "You just gave us a reason to act tough. We don't have time to be nice! Get into your space suits, we're going to open that barrel up like a slice of cake, and take her."

Abe reached out a long arm and pulled Sylvy away from me and the radio. "Stall him some more, Joey. Negotiate." Ma nodded.

I pushed the send button. "My ma says she'll negotiate with you for better work for Miss Saint Clair. She should sign a contract for doing something else she likes better."

The radio sputtered and blurbled. "Our terms. Damn, something . . . burble . . . We were sent to bring the gurble back, not negotiate no curble, gurble." It turned to a frying noise.

I figure the syrup had gotten to them and was sticking up their radio antenna surfaces. Abe let out a big last dose of syrup as we spun around again, and we could see the spaceboat wasn't shiny any more. It was covered with streaks of sticky-looking foam. The syrup was foaming in space, and drying out to something like crunch molasses candy, on the boat, all over its view lenses. There isn't much in the world that will dissolve hard molasses.

After a while of us watching, the boat started going slowly around and around like a pinwheel, so the molasses was into something else.

Abe took a special laser rig we had in a back locker, and recorded a *help* message on it with our orbit coordinates and the story about the men from the gambling place, Jason's Emporium, and what they'd done to our house. He set it up outside the airlock to track the signal radio flashes from the Belt Foundry and flash back.

About an hour later two very big, tough tractor tugs armed with front-end cutters and handlers arrived and hovered on our view screens like giant lobsters. They talked with Abe. I mean the engineers in them talked with Abe while we kids danced around and begged for a ride inside a tug. Then the tugs sliced off all the gun barrels that were sticking out of the spaceboat and one tug towed the spaceboat off toward Jason's Emporium and the other engineer stayed and said he'd take Abe and Sylvy off toward the Belt Foundry to get married.

The engineer explained to Abe that the Foundry would loan him money to buy Sylvy's contract from the gambling hall. They said that other men had had to buy their wives' contracts. The company had gotten used to giving out loans for a man to get a wife. Besides, they needed girls over at the Foundry to do office and thinking type work and brighten the place up. Sylvy could get a job there. They said everybody at the Belt Foundry agreed they needed to have more women around.

She and Abe went off together and left the place kind of empty, but after a while the piglets started chasing each other around faster than ever and we started laughing and the place seemed crowded enough after all.

Ma lets me visit Abe and my new sister Sylvy almost every weekend. The Belt Foundry living barrel is so big it has three floor levels, each with a different gravity and a gymnasium with zero G to fly in at the center. Abe won't let me look into the men's lounge because he promised Ma, but I look in sometimes while I'm waiting for him and Sylvy to come down from their room, and I see men playing cards, and Ping-Pong and pool, and drinking and laughing and watching a huge screen video and telly. And every time a commercial comes on it's either advertising Sam's Spacesuits or Jason's Emporium, Turkish Bath, Massage and Fun Palace. When it advertises Jason's Emporium where Sylvy came from, it always shows pictures of lots of girls dancing, wearing nothing but jewelry and long beautiful hair like Sylvy when I first saw her.

When Abe and Sylvy came down Abe looked very happy, but he pulled me away from the door to the lounge. He said he promised Ma. Ma won't even let

Harriet come visit at all. She has to stay home, even though she's fifteen and I'm only eleven. I guess there's some advantage in being a man.

When I grow up and get a job at Belt Foundry, I'll go to Jason's Emporium, like Abe did, and rescue a girl.

I'm studying hard to be an Engineer.

Invasion Report

by Theodore R. Cogswell

It was a great victory for the kids, but it's not clear whether suppertime or sticking to their guns was most important.

Colonel William Faust of the Solar Guard had no business being where he was at the moment.

He took his wide, leather belt in another notch and eyed himself critically. First, gleaming space boots, then, flaring breeches of midnight black and finally, a soft, snug-fitting, high-collared tunic with the insignia of the Guard which was a crimson lightning flash running diagonally across the front.

On Vega III, the light cruiser Andros of the Imperial Legion hurtled up through the thin atmosphere. . . .

The Colonel's hands caressed the smooth butts of the snub-nosed weapons that hung at each hip and then slid away to hang carelessly at his sides. He turned his back to the hatch that led into the control room of

93

the *Glorious*, took two casual steps and then, without warning, spun around as his hands went streaking for his guns. A split-second later, he stood catlike, poised on the balls of his feet, both guns trained steadily on the glaring image of himself that was reflected in the mirror surface of the port.

On Vega III, the light cruiser Andros of the Imperial Legion hurtled up through the thin atmosphere on a mission of interstellar conquest. . . .

"Faster than ever," said the warlike figure with stern satisfaction and then, holstering his weapons and adjusting his dress helmet to a jaunty angle, he threw open the hatch that led into the control room of the *Glorious* and entered with a measured military stride.

Somebody barked, "Attention!" and ten sets of heels clicked together. Captain Shirey stepped forward and saluted. "All present and accounted for, sir."

The owners of the ten sets of heels had no more business being where they were than did their Colonel. The starship *Glorious* had GOVERNMENT PROPERTY— KEEP OUT painted in foot-high letters on one side of her main entrance port and TRESPASSERS WILL BE PROSECUTED on the other—warnings that had been blithely ignored by the guard when the headlights of the battered old flyer that had brought them out blinked out the three shorts and three longs that activated the landing lock.

For a few years after her return from Alpha Centauri, a small maintenance crew had been kept on the

Glorious. But as existence became more and more peaceful and settled and Man slowly adjusted to the idea that there was no longer any place to go, these were withdrawn until, finally, the last watchman was removed as being an unnecessary charge against the public funds.

There was talk, for a while, of mounting a warper on her and turning her into a museum, but nobody was really interested except the youngsters—and youngsters don't have votes—so it was finally decided to leave her circling in her lonely orbit as a perpetual monument to the men who had taken her out for the first and last time.

"At ease!" As his command relaxed, Colonel Faust stepped out of role.

"Look here, gang," he said, "we've worked through those old operational manuals of my grandfather's until we know them backward. I figure it's about time we put some of what we know to work. What would you think of the idea of turning on the big vision screen?"

Captain Shirey looked at him dubiously. "To run the scanners, you've got to have power—and that means turning on the main pile."

"So what, Wimpy? All we have to do is just like the manuals say. We've done it a dozen times in dry runs."

The other still looked doubtful. "If you make a mistake when you're just pretending, nothing blows up. And anyway, just being up here would get us in enough trouble, if anybody caught us. If we start turning things on and maybe break something, then we'd really catch it. Why can't we just keep on pretending the same way we have been?"

"Because," said his commander patiently, "you can only learn so much by pretending—and we've learned all we can that way. We've got to get some practice done on the real thing if we're going to be ready when the invaders come. There won't be any pretending then, not when you got to stand back and watch your own sister being dragged off to be a slave. You just think about that for a while."

Wimpy dutifully began to think about it but, somehow, the only reaction he could get to the idea of his sister being stolen was one of relief rather than regret. "They take old Emily, they'll be sorry," he said finally.

Bill started to nod agreement, then caught himself. "Look," he said, "four times now we've sneaked out my father's old flyer while he was out of town and slipped up here—and all we've done is pretend. We got to start really running things if we're going to get trained right. The invaders come in and who else is going to stop them? Those pooping, little police boats with a ten-mile ceiling and maybe one medium paralyzer on them?"

Wimpy still looked doubtful.

"You let me do the worrying," said Bill. "I got more right to be here than most people."

Halfway between Earth and Venus there was a sudden shimmer as the Vegan ship slipped out of warp

*into normal space. It hung motionless for a minute
as the alien commander checked his instruments and
his armament.*

Looking at it one way, William Faust did have more
right than most to be on board the *Glorious*. In his
room at home, under his bed, was his great-grand-
father's space chest. In it lay the worn diary that recorded the first high hopes when the *Glorious* took
off, then the boredom, then the bitterness and disil-
lusionment that came when Alpha Centauri was found
to be a barren and lifeless system.

Bill Faust knew it almost by heart, that chronicle
of the young man who went out on the first—and last—
starship ever to be constructed, of the middle-aged
man who arrived, of the old man who returned to find
space-flight a thing of the past and the reports of the
expedition that had consumed his life used as final
proof of the DeWitt hypothesis that there could be no
life on other systems.

There had been a time when those whose dreams
were strong enough to stand the shock of crossing over
into what adults called "the real world" had some place
to go, once they reached the other side. For these,
being young was a time of waiting and training for the
day when new strength could be tested against whatever lay beyond the safe frontiers. First, seas and
continents, then the upper air and the pushing of limits
toward the Moon, the planets, until, these once con-

quered, young eyes turned toward the beckoning beacons of the distant stars themselves.

There had been such a time, but it existed no longer. With the coming of the warpers—those strange contraptions that could so twist the fabric of space that Man and his materials could instantaneously be moved from any place where there was a transmitter to any other where there was a receiver—Mars and Venus were nearer than the corner drugstore. Once they had been set up, space-flight died. There was no point in spending months traveling from one planet to another when one could do it in a fraction of a second, merely by stepping in one door and out the other.

The one star that could be reached had been reached. The *Glorious* had returned to slam shut the last gateway to adventure. As for the other stars, they were distant lonely things that hung so far out of reach that only astronomers any longer viewed them with more than casual interest. The great mathematicians and physicists had proved so conclusively that a faster-than-light drive was impossible, nobody bothered to check their figures any longer.

Life was snug and easy and pleasant—and, above all, sensible. Only the youngsters still dreamed of danger and the search for strange things in far places. And, since the best of the psychologists said that a temporary sojourn into a world of make-believe was important to the growing process, the young ones were permitted to assume such strange warlike disguises as were necessary to take them into imaginary worlds of high adventure—providing, of course, that they weren't too noisy about it and emerged in time for supper with clean hands and clean faces. . . .

"Check pile controls!" As usual, Colonel Faust had won his point.

"All on full safety, sir," said Second Lieutenant Randolph with a most unmilitary quaver in his voice. He was the most junior of the junior officers, a precocious nine-year-old who was four or five years younger than the rest of the Guardsmen and he had an unfortunate habit of bursting into tears during moments of stress. He was already sniffing slightly, when Bill came over to check the control positions against the diagram he'd memorized.

With a curt nod of approval, Colonel Faust went over to his position at the coordination board and grasped the red handle of the master pile control.

"Power on!"

He pulled back slowly until the lever clicked into the normal operation slot. In the pile room of the *Glorious*, control rods slid smoothly back until they were checked by the safety catches. There was a faint hum of transformers as the long-neglected ship warmed to life.

"Battle screen on!"

A Guardsman frowned in concentration and slowly began to throw the switches that linked the great screen with the scanners set in the outer hull. There was a flicker and then a few tiny white spots blinked on to show meteors large enough to be detected. But, aside from these, there was nothing to show that the screen had been powered.

Colonel Faust gave a grunt of satisfaction, rose to his feet and faced his Guardsmen.

"Your attention, gentlemen," he said in a tone of command.

Ten grim-faced Guardsmen leaned forward expectantly as he pointed dramatically to the empty screen.

"As you can see, the Plutonian fleet is approaching in a cone formation with their heaviest ships at the tip. These are carrying a deadly new weapon, the Q-ray. Our mission is to break through the cone and destroy the flagship, from which the Warlord of Pluto is personally directing the operations of his fleet. Earth expects every man to do his duty." He paused and then barked, *"Engage!"*

The Guardsmen hunched at their positions as their imaginations suddenly populated the empty screen with a hurtling cone of enemy ships.

Many were the fierce encounters in the next few hours, and close were the brushes with death. When the *Glorious* tore through the outer cone of Plutonian ships and came within range of the shimmering web of Q-rays, the Guardsmen reacted to the fiery touch in quite different fashions. Their Colonel had invented the new weapon on the spur of the moment, and there had been no chance for agreement as to just what its effects would be.

Bill remained seated at the coordination board, his face set in a mask of heroic and Promethean suffering. Wimpy, on the other hand, went threshing around on the control room floor, howling that his skin was coming off and that his bones were turning to limp and rubbery things. The rest of the Guards were so impressed by his performance that it wasn't long before the whole contingent, Bill included, were writhing on the floor like wounded snakes.

"The Warlord is making a run for it!" Colonel Faust's voice rang through the general hubbub. "We've got to intercept him. *Stations!*"

Deaf to all but the call of duty, the dying Guardsmen summoned up strength from some hidden reserve and crawled painfully back to their posts on the supposedly rotting stumps of what once had been arms and legs. Colonel Faust fought for five minutes before he was able to reach the master controls. A wavering cheer went up as they once more began to creep up on the ship of the tyrant. He fought back desperately, his great guns hammering shot after shot into the *Glorious*, but still the gallant ship drove on, her mighty drive tubes incandescent under the overload.

"Prepare to ram!"

As the *Glorious* went into her final dive, the game was suddenly terminated by a harsh clangor from the proximity alarm and a red dot jumped into being in the upper left corner of the vision screen. As it crawled toward the center, alarm after alarm went off until the control room was filled with a clanging din.

"Shut those things off!" yelled Bill. Jimmie Ozaki, the Guardsman at the detection station, kicked over a series of switches and the noise suddenly stopped.

"What is it?"

Jimmie stared at the instruments in front of him, as if he'd never seen them before. "If I'm reading these things right, whatever it is would be about fifteen thousand miles out and coming in fast. It just popped up out of no place. So I guess I'm not reading these things right."

Bill went over and made a quick check. "You are."

"Couldn't be a meteor, could it?" asked Wimpy.

Bill shook his head. "If it was, it would show up as a white dot. Red indicates radiation of some sort. The only thing I can figure out is that somebody is out there in a flyer."

"Ain't no flyer can travel that fast," objected Ozaki. "And how come it popped up like it did? Even if it were coasting along with its drive off, its mass would still have registered on the detectors."

Bill stared up at the screen uneasily. "Could be that the scanners are out of kilter somehow. You keep checking, Jimmie."

Five minutes later, it was reported as being only a hundred miles away and slowing rapidly. And then Jimmie Ozaki let out a sudden yell. "It's hitting us with some sort of a high frequency beam. Looks as if it might be in the communication band."

"Try and tune it in, but don't answer."

The Guardsman at the communication station leaned over his controls. A moment later a speaker came to life. A hissing stream of sibilants came from it, sounds like nothing that had ever been produced by human vocal apparatus. The message was repeated twice and then the speaker went silent. So did the Guardsmen.

Bill was the first to speak. There was a nervous smile on his face when he did. "It must be a police boat," he said in a strained voice. "They must of spotted us sneaking up here, and they're trying to throw a scare into us. We're in for it, now."

"That's no police boat, and you know it," whispered Wimpy. "The flyers they got couldn't go out that far, even if they wanted to."

"It's moving in again."

Bill swung quickly to the detection station. "Can you pick that up on visual?"

"I'll try."

The detection screen blanked out for a minute, then lit up again to show a silver speck hanging in darkness.

"Crank her up!"

As power was thrown into the magnifiers, the strange ship swelled in size until it filled half the screen, a gleaming sphere that was like nothing that was recognizable.

"Still think that's a police boat?" said Wimpy in a strained voice.

Bill didn't answer. He watched in horrified fascination as the strange ship hurtled toward the *Glorious*.

It looked as if it were on a collision course, but it suddenly began to decelerate and then, finally, curved into a path that put it in orbit around the *Glorious*.

"How close now?"

Ozaki, at the detection station, had trouble getting his eyes off the screen long enough to read his instruments.

"Less than a mile," he said finally.

"What now?" squeaked somebody.

Nobody had an immediate answer. The Guardsmen looked at each other and then at the suddenly strange control room, where everything now seemed to be constructed on a scale several sizes too large for them. It was a place for men, not for boys. They all turned to Bill and waited for him to say something.

For a moment, he couldn't. He was being pulled in two directions at once. Panic tugged at him, panic that threatened momentarily to seize control of his legs and send him bolting to the safety of the old flyer that sat in the landing lock. Against this urge to flee was the dawning realization that they were no longer playing a game which could be discontinued at will. It was like a nightmare where one has suddenly lost the saving knowledge that he can always wake up if things get too bad.

To run or to stand, to retreat from grim reality or to face it—the decision had to be made. Bill was standing on the line that separates the child from the man, and he had to move one way or the other. He looked

at the menacing shape on the screen, then at the frightened faces of the other boys who were waiting for him
to take the lead.

He dropped his eyes, and it seemed as if the deck
plates beneath his feet had turned to glass, so that he
could see the smug, defenseless world that stretched
out below. A tidy, rational world that had long ago
given up such childish things as arms and armies—
and spaceships. When he finally spoke, his voice was
so low they could hardly hear him.

"We've got to stay," he said.

When the words penetrated, there was a shuffling
of feet and a muttering of disagreement. "We shouldn't
have come out here in the first place!" said Wimpy.

Second Lieutenant Randolph began to sniffle. "I want
to go home," he announced. "Right now!"

"Me too," said Ozaki, "and I'm going. Let's get out
of here before it's too late." He started to sidle toward
the door. The rest wavered, then began to follow him.

Bill hesitated only a moment, then dashed across
the control room and slammed the door shut. *"Wait!"*
he shouted, throwing himself in front of it. "It's already
too late. You can't get away now."

Captain Shirey forgot about military courtesy and
cocked one hard fist under his superior's nose. "You
get out of the way, or you're going to get a bust on
the snoot!"

"You've *got* to listen to me," said Bill frantically.
"That thing's only a mile away from us, and we're three

hundred miles out from Earth. You saw how fast it can go. If it's looking for trouble, do you think it's just going to sit by and let us pull away in that old flyer?"

Wimpy started to answer and then stopped. He let his fist drop slowly to his side. "Maybe you're right," he said slowly. "But if we don't run, then what?"

"Just sit for a while and see what happens. From the way that ship's acting, they must figure the *Glorious* has been abandoned. They'd never have come this close, if they didn't. If they're just snooping around and don't catch on that anybody's in here, maybe they'll just go away."

There were wistful glances toward the door, but after a moment the whole contingent straggled back to their positions.

As they watched the alien ship, a square hatch opened in its gleaming spherical hull. There was a suggestion of movement and then a long, torpedo-shaped object slowly emerged and floated free alongside the ship. There was something seated on it—something that wasn't human! It wore a wheel-shaped spacesuit with a hemispherical vision dome bulging out from the center.

There was a little spurt of flame from the rear of the torpedo, and then it sped away from the alien ship, twisting and looping about. The thing riding on it moved busily for a moment, adjusting the controls. Then he brought it to a halt with its nose pointing toward the *Glorious*.

"What do you think they're figuring on doing with that?" asked Wimpy in a shaky voice.

"Using it on us."

"What for?"

"How many other spaceships does Earth have? Once the *Glorious* is knocked out, there's nothing left that can be used against them."

"But this thing can't fight," protested Wimpy. "And there's nobody left that knows how to run her."

"She could fight once," said Bill grimly. "Maybe she still can. And there is somebody left to run her—us!" He turned his back to the screen and snapped, *"Stations!"* The Guard slowly took on a semblance of order.

"All positions on. And I mean really on! We aren't playing any longer. I want an immediate report on the condition of this tub."

There was hesitation for a moment, then a sudden flurry of action at each position as switches were thrown and instruments read. When they came, the reports weren't very encouraging.

"All drives disconnected."

The *Glorious* couldn't run away.

"No missiles in the racks."

"No shells in the lockers."

The *Glorious* couldn't fight.

"There's got to be *something*," said Bill as he went over to the gunnery station. The Guardsman at the controls looked up unhappily and pointed to the long row of little red plates that registered the number of

rounds available for each gun. Each was blinking out
the word EMPTY. "Turrets and automatic trackers are
still operational, but that doesn't help any."

Bill stood thinking a minute. "Maybe it can," he said
finally and went back to the coordination board. "Look,
gang," he said. "What we know and what they know are
two different things. They've no way of knowing that
those guns aren't loaded. Maybe we can pull a bluff."

"And if we can't?" said somebody.

He shrugged. "Somebody got a better idea? We can't
just sit here and let them blow up the ship."

Wimpy let out a sudden shout and pointed toward
the screen. Bill spun around and saw the alien was
leaving the torpedo and returning to his ship. He felt
a sudden dryness in his throat.

"This is it!" he yelled. "All guns on target!"

There was a growl of powerful motors as the turrets,
set in blisters along the top and sides of the *Glorious*,
swung swiftly to zero in their long-muzzled guns on
the alien ship. There was no reaction for a moment,
and then a long burst of sound came from the wall
speakers.

"Do you want to answer that?"

Bill shook his head. "Better if we don't talk. Maybe
they've got some sort of a translator over there. If I
start shooting off my mouth, I might say the wrong
thing."

"*Bill!*" There was a shout from the detection station.

"Yeah?" He didn't look away from the screen. The

torpedo still hung motionless, its nose pointed toward the *Glorious*.

"I think they're trying to make visual contact."

"See if you can pick them up," Bill ordered.

There was a flickering in the reproduction cube of the tri-V receiver and, slowly, a distorted replica of the control room of the alien ship began to materialize. Then, as the Guardsman at the communication station struggled with his controls, the scene cleared.

There were seven of them. They weren't humanoid—they looked like huge, furry footballs—but they weren't the slavering monstrosities that Bill and the rest had half expected.

"Turn on our transmitter."

After a brief warm-up period, there was a bouncing of aliens and their own screen lit up. Bill stepped forward, and as sternly as he could, made a stabbing motion toward Earth with a bent forefinger. There was a small commotion while all the fur balls rolled together to form a huddle. Then one of them went bouncing over to a set of controls at the far end of their control room.

"The bluff didn't work," gasped Wimpy. "They're going to blast us with that torp!"

"Not yet," said Bill. "Gunnery!"

"Yes?"

"Automatic trackers on!"

The Guardsman at the gunnery station looked puzzled, but he didn't ask any questions. His hands slid

forward and the parabolic mirrors that projected the
UHF beams—that had once controlled the guided missiles carried by the *Glorious*—swung until they were
centered on the silver sphere.

"Carriers on!"

"Check."

There was a sudden flurry of movement in the alien
control rooms as their detectors gave warning of the
beams that were striking their hull. Bill faced the tri-
V scanner and held up his hand for attention. There
was some more scuttling and then all the aliens faced
toward their own screen. Bill withdrew one of the odd-
shaped weapons that hung at his hip and held it up so
they could see it.

"Get over here, Wimpy."

"What for?"

"Hurry up. And play it straight."

The freckle-faced second in command marched over
with a military stride and saluted.

"Q-ray," said Bill. "Get it?"

Wimpy started to protest and then caught himself.
"Sounds crazy to me," he muttered, "but you're the
boss."

Bill's side-arm was a complicated affair with two
short barrels, one capped with a green lens and the
other with a red. He held the weapon out to call attention to it and then raised it and pressed a stud on
the stock three times. Three bursts of red light flared
out briefly.

"Give them three quick flips on the missile beams."
The Guardsman hit the cut-off button one, two, three.
Bill's gun flashed red three more times.
"Once more should give them the idea."
Again the carrier beams were clicked on and off.
"Make this good." Bill pointed the weapon deliberately at Wimpy and pressed the stud. Captain Shirey stood at attention, a circle of red light glowing on his chest.
"Now!" There was a sudden green flash as Bill jerked the other trigger.
Immediately Wimpy let out a bloodcurdling yell and then, clawing at his chest, collapsed in a writhing heap on the floor. Bill turned back to the scanner and pointed to his gun again.
"Three more." By the time the barrier beams had struck the other ship twice, chaos had let loose in its control room.
"What's happening?"
It was hard to tell. They were lined up in a row, their pink underbodies tilted toward the ceiling, and weak, little leglike organs waving wildly.
"I think," said Colonel Faust slowly, "that they're standing on their heads."
But surrender was not negotiated without some difficulty. The alien who seemed to be the commander kept bouncing in and out of one of a pair of metallic cups which projected from a complex mechanism at one side of the control room. Bill finally got the idea.

"I think they've got some sort of a mechanical translator and they want me to come over."

There was a protest from the floor. "You can't go there!"

"Shut up!" said Bill. "You're supposed to be dead. Do you want to give the whole show away?" Wimpy subsided obediently. "I've got to go over. We can't escort them down and, once they find out that we aren't following, there's nothing to keep them from making a run for it. I'll take the flyer over. There's a three-quarter-size pressure suit in the luggage compartment that I think I can get into. Keep me covered."

"With what?" softly mumbled Wimpy.

Later, with one exception, the Solar Guard stood at attention as a small red dot crawled toward one corner of the detection screen.

"Can I get up now?" said a plaintive voice.

Colonel Bill Faust looked down at the sprawled form of his second in command and then suddenly doubled up and began to emit strangled sounds that were half sobs and half laughter. He finally recovered enough to reach down and pull Wimpy to his feet.

"You were real good, Wimpy. Real good!" He went off into another hysterical paroxysm.

Wimpy grabbed him by the shoulders and shook him. "*Stop* it! Why did you let them go?"

"They—they . . ." Bill choked, gasped and then tried again. "They couldn't stay any longer. They had to get home for supper."

"They *what?*" gasped Wimpy.

"They had to get home for supper." Bill pointed at the screen. "And there they go."

Faster, the red dot went, and faster still, and then it flicked out of sight.

"I'll bet that's the last time they come snooping around the Reservation," said Bill with a mysterious grin.

"The what?"

"The Reservation. That's this whole star cluster."

Wimpy advanced purposefully and waved a fist threateningly. "Are you going to tell us what happened, or do we have to beat it out of you?"

Bill worked hard to control himself. "Suppose," he said at last, "that, aside from a few dead systems like Alpha Centauri, the Universe was full of life—and some of the races have had interstellar drives for so long that even the kids' flyers are equipped with them." He looked around at the boys.

"Go ahead," said Wimpy impatiently.

"Don't you get it?"

They all stared at him blankly.

"Well," he continued, "suppose a bunch of kids were out one day, and they went poking around where they had no business being, and they found a big old ship that looked deserted."

"The *Glorious!*"

"So, whenever they could get away, they'd sneak over and play invasion."

"Oh, no!" said Wimpy.

"And then, one day, they decided to run a real all-out offensive, and one of the kids borrowed his father's ship without bothering to ask permission. And right in the middle of the game, the turrets on the ship they thought was deserted suddenly swing around, and they find a couple of dozen space-rifles pointed directly at them. They want to run away, but they're too scared, and to make matters worse, they get a demonstration of a horrible, strange weapon. And we thought *we* were scared!"

There was silence in the control room for a moment as the Guardsmen tried to digest what had happened.

"But what about the torpedo?" asked Wimpy.

Bill patted the elaborate toy that hung at his right hip. "It had as much real punch as this. They were making believe that it was a vortex torpedo—they'd rigged it up with remote controls—but it was really only one of the little flyers that they turn out for the kids over there. It's an old one, but its interstellar drive is still working."

He paused, then said in an offhand manner, "I brought it back with me. It's got an adjustable warp field that'll open up wide enough to handle a ship the size of the *Glorious*, and I—well, it seemed to me that, maybe, it might get space travel going. . . ."

It did.

A Start in Life

by Arthur Sellings

Like Adam and Eve, these children tasted the apple of knowledge, and life was never quite the same.

"C-A-T spells Cat," said Em.

"But what *is* a cat?" said Paul.

"Why, here's a cat. Look at his big striped tail."

But Paul only pushed the book away petulantly. "I want a cat. A real cat I can pull the tail of."

"Cats aren't made for you to pull their tails," said Em. "Now, C-A-T spells—"

"Cat, *cat*, CAT!" he wailed, kicking his little heels on the floor.

Em hesitated, then returned to her task. "Very well. *The cat sat on the mat.* M-A-T, Mat. And here's a mat." She held it up. "A *real* mat."

Paul sniffed contemptuously and, with a child's unanswerable logic, said, "How can you say what a cat's made for and what a cat's not made for, if we haven't got a cat?"

If Em had been human, she would have sighed. As
it was, she wondered whether the child's question was
good or bad. It was good because it showed power of
reasoning; bad because it might get in the way of his
studies. Helen now was different. She just listened
and repeated the words, but Em was never sure whether
she really understood.

"Why *can't* I have a real cat, Em?" said Paul. "In
the book, the boy's got a cat. Why can't *I* have a cat,
a real alive cat, not one in a book? An alive cat, same
as we're alive."

In the web of Em's mind floated several thoughts.
One was that she wasn't really alive—not *really*. And
that brought the feeling of something a human would
have called pain. It wasn't pain, though, but something
worse, because a robot couldn't feel pain. Another was
that it was bad enough as it was, having to teach them
from books showing children in circumstances that they
themselves knew nothing of; having to avoid their
questions, putting them off and off—

"In the story Jay was reading me the other bedtime,
they buyed a cat in a shop. Why can't *we* buy a cat in
a shop!" He screwed up his face and added in a plaintive little voice, "And how do you *buy*?"

Really, thought Em, she would have to have a word
with Jay and suggest that he be more careful about
what he read to them. He was too good-natured, too
easy-going.

"How do you *buy*?" Paul said again, tugging at her metal kneejoint.

"Well, it's giving something for something else. Like . . ." She floundered. It *did* involve giving something for something else. She'd heard the grown-ups mention it—in the days when there had been grown-ups. They had joked about it the way humans did joke, because here buying and—what was it?—selling had no meaning.

"It isn't important," she said.

"What's important?"

"That you learn your lessons."

"No, I mean what does *important* mean?"

"If you learn your lessons, you'll learn what important means." As she said it she realized it couldn't be very convincing, especially to a six-year-old. So she added hastily, "You'll learn what all the long words mean, and then you'll be able to read all the books there are. All the big books with long words in them."

To her surprise, the mention of big books did not brighten his eyes as it always had before.

"They're all lies!" he burst out. "I don't want to learn anything. They're all lies about things that don't happen. There ain't such things as cats and trees and—and . . ." He broke into bitter sobbing.

"Not ain't—*aren't*," said Em, cursing herself the next moment. As if that really mattered when there were only the four of them. She reached out a hand to comfort him. But he shrugged it away.

"Come on," she said, trying to modulate her voice like a human, trying to be soft and gentle and comforting and knowing that she couldn't manage it. "We do have trees, anyway."

He looked up, his face flushed and indignant. "They're not trees," he retorted vehemently. "They're only a lot of old weeds. You can climb up *real* trees."

"I thought you said those were lies in the books about trees," she said. This time she did manage to get a whisper into her voice so that he would understand that she was only kidding him—she hoped.

But he only burst into a renewed fit of sobbing.

"There *are* trees," she persisted. "Leastways, there have been trees. And there will be again." She didn't like to think what the odds were against that, so she didn't. "I've seen them with my own eyes. You believe Em, don't you?" She put out her hand again, and this time he did not reject it. He threw himself into her hard, cold, metallic lap.

"Oh, Em," he sobbed. "Oh, Em!" But his tears now were not the tears of anger and separation, but of union in a common loss, so that Em, too, might have wept had she been human.

Instead she ran her clumsy, inadequate fingers through his damp, blond hair, and said, "There, *there*," but this time it was far too loud and mechanical, so she stopped talking and cradled him in her arms, rocking him till his weeping subsided.

She was still rocking him when Jay came back from the gardens with Helen.

Bursting through the doorway, Helen yelled excitedly, "Look what I've got. A flower! A real flower!"

"*Sh-sh*," said Em in a whisper like a steam valve going off.

"Oh," said Helen, "can't I wake him to show him my flower?" She held the sickly yellowish bloom in front of her face.

"No," said Em, "he's tired. I shouldn't have given him an extra lesson." She turned to Jay. "What is this flower?"

"It just grew, Em," said Jay. "I found it in the beds along with the plants."

"Jay, is that the truth?"

It wasn't conscience that made Jay shake his head, but knowing that Em *knew* the truth. "*I*—I planted a couple of seeds. One of the seed bags in the stores was split open and I found the seeds on the floor. It won't do any harm, Em."

"I thought we agreed that nothing like that must be touched. We don't know what might happen."

"Don't worry about it, Em. I read all about it in a book before I planted them. I thought the children ought to have something. They get so little—"

"Don't you think it's time to put the children to bed?" said Em warningly. She noticed that Helen had hidden the pitiful flower behind her back.

"Sure, sure," said Jay. "But about these seeds, Em. I thought perhaps we could . . ."

He faltered. Neither robot had anything like facial muscles with which to express a meaning without words, but the way Em was looking at him now—head lowered, shining eyes leveled at him from beneath her rounded brow—was warning enough.

"All right, Em. Let me have the boy. Come along, Helen. Bedtime."

But Helen did not turn. She looked up at Em. "I may keep the flower, Em, mayn't I?"

"Of course, Helen," said Em after only a moment's hesitation. If any harm had been done, it was done by now. "I'll put some water in a glass and you can have it near your bed. How's that?"

"Oh, thank you, Em, *thank* you!" She rushed over and clasped Em about the legs. Em lifted her gently up, but held her at arm's length. Otherwise, she knew, the child would kiss her, for she was more demonstrative than the boy. And the thought that she was all in the nature of a mother the child had to kiss—only cold unyielding metal—made Em feel inadequate. And whether she was supposed to be able to feel that or not, she did—and too often.

As she set Helen down, Em noticed the disappointed expression that always came when she had to frustrate her childlike impulses. But the look she gave Em before she turned to follow Jay was somehow different from any Em had noticed before.

Em stood there looking after her for quite a long time. In fact, she was still looking after her, standing in the same awkward, unhuman stance, when Jay returned. As he sat down, she sat down in the chair facing him. Sitting was another habit they'd long ago acquired from humans and not relinquished when the humans had died.

Jay stirred. "Helen didn't want to hear a story tonight," he said.

"Oh?" she said. There was a long pause.

"Em," he said at last. "You're not really mad at me, are you? About the flowers, I mean."

"I think you're a fool, that's all," she said. "We can't afford to take risks like that. Germs, spores—we just don't know what might come from something new."

"But we inoculated them against everything, didn't we? Don't you remember, Em? Didn't I hold them when you put the needle in?"

"Oh, *stop* it," she said crossly. Of course she remembered. How could she forget? Those first years when there had been so many things to remember from the last hurried instructions. How to change and bathe babies with hands that had never been made for it. How to nurse them through the childhood ailments that came in spite of all the inoculations. How to teach things that had never been taught to oneself, because they'd either been unnecessary or built in.

Nervous breakdown couldn't happen to a robot, because a robot's system wasn't like a human's. But bringing up a human baby was an almost hopeless task for a robot, Em thought. One mental image had become a recurring and fearful one—the fantastic image of herself exploding under the strain, of cogs and springs and synthetic brain-cells flying in all directions.

That was the image that came back now to frighten and confound her.

It was different with Jay. She looked at him as he sat there, silent after the sharpness of her admonition. Her mind went back to the first days, the very first days before this great burden of responsibility had been laid upon them.

How carefree it had been then! The way, for instance, the humans had come to treat her and Jay like male and female. It was only coincidence that Jay's prefix made a man's name and hers a woman's. Being an earlier model, which accounted for the alphabetical precedence, he *was* clumsier, bulkier, squarer, while she was neater, smaller, more agile and more smoothly shaped. More delicate of voice, too. But besides, she had a quicker intuition than his, a more gentle manner and certainly a greater tendency to worry. It had been he who had joined in the jokes of the men, trying to understand them, dancing clumsy dances to amuse everyone when spirits were low. Meanwhile, she had learned to cook, although it was no more part of her job than dancing was his.

In human company they had gradually assumed the positions of man and wife—he boasting sometimes of being older and more experienced, she slyly pointing out that that didn't make him necessarily wiser. He, since the last human grown-ups had all gone, thinking more of making the children happy—she of keeping them safe.

And, like a wife who knows she is more intelligent than her husband, she tried to use it by not demonstrating it too often. But now she felt she had to speak.

"If anything ever happens to them we'll be *alone*. I don't think you properly realize just how delicate human beings are."

"Of course I do, Em."

"And not only in their bodies," she went on, as if she hadn't heard him. "You'll have to be more careful what you read to them."

"Now what have I done?"

"Don't read them any stories about children having things *they* can't have. Stick to fairy stories."

"But there aren't many fairy stories. They know them all by heart now. Anyway, humans wouldn't have had these books for the children if they were bad for them, would they?"

"*Oh, oh, oh!* Sometimes I wonder what goes on inside that big square head of yours. Don't you see that it wouldn't matter if they had their own mothers and fathers to tell them?"

"Of course I see. I just didn't think that—"

"Well, think, then," she said sharply.

He lowered his gaze. "I do think," he said after a pause. Then he looked up and said, "I think, for instance, that before long we'll just have to tell them. The truth, I mean."

"Why do you say that now?" she said, suddenly fearful.

"Oh, just things they say sometimes. The way they ask about the big door, the way their eyes stray toward it. Little things like that."

"I know," Em said at length, "but I'm frightened. Frightened about how they'll take it, about what knowing will do to them."

They were silent for long minutes. Then Jay said, "Can't *we* invent a fairy story? One big fairy story about everything, so that we never have to tell them the truth."

Em laid her metal hand on his. "Dear Jay. Can you invent even a *little* fairy story?"

He shook his head dumbly.

"And neither can I," said Em. "Even if we could, it wouldn't last long. It would only be one long evasion, instead of the little evasions we make now. And anyhow, in two or three years they'll have the strength to open the big door themselves. And we won't be able to stop them. They've got to learn by then. They should understand enough of the little truths so that the big truth won't be too great a shock to them."

"Well, for my part," said Jay, "I don't see how learning that C-A-T spells Cat or that two and two bolts make four would prepare them."

"Of course you wouldn't," she said and her tone was sharp again. Because she knew that, in his

simple, direct way, he had come closer to the truth
than she cared to admit. "It's a question of de-
veloping their minds. Disciplining them. Preparing
them."

"It was only a thought," said Jay hastily. "You know
best, Em. You always do."

But it became evident to Em before very long that
one *couldn't* teach the small truths if one kept dodging
the big one all the time. For the children's growing
puzzlement blocked their will to learn.

They were still struggling through the first-year lessons of a five-year-old. Em studied the teaching manuals through the long hours while the children were
asleep, trying to perfect herself as a teacher, trying
to find out where she had gone wrong.

Their minds were keen enough. Their questions didn't
abate. They became more subtle, more suddenly sprung
in the attempt to get past the tightening mesh of their
guardians' evasions. And it became increasingly clear
to Em that each evasion was a step backward.

She tried answering their questions in meaningless
polysyllables and, when they pressed for explanations,
telling them that there was no easier way of putting
it, that only by learning would they be able to understand. *That* device she gave up for they soon came to
see through it. She could tell by the look that came
into their faces—the by now familiar look of hurt mis-
trust.

The crux came when Paul asked a question she just

couldn't avoid answering. It was a question that every child asks his mother sooner or later, but Em didn't know that. Her awkwardness when he suddenly asked her in the middle of a tediously slow arithmetic lesson, "Em, where did I come from?" was not of the same kind that an ill-prepared mother might feel. But it *was* awkward, none the less.

Her first impulse was to hedge, telling him not to ask general questions during class. But one look at his anxious little face stopped her. She was also aware of Helen's gaze upon her, a half-smile on her lips, but the rest of her face set, obdurate—and yes, accusing.

"Why," she said, "well . . ."

Jay was there and she looked at him for help, even knowing that he could not give it. The helpless gesture he made with his hands was unnecessary.

"Helen says," said Paul, "that a big machine made us. She says that sometimes she can hear it throbbing. She says that when it's throbbing it's making babies."

Oh, no, thought Em, *not this!* This wasn't right at all. They couldn't be allowed to think like that. Machines were not the masters. Men made machines. A machine could never make men. But how else could they be expected to think? Wasn't it natural when they knew no other humans, when two machines controlled their lives?

"Do you believe that, Helen?" she asked. But Helen only dropped her eyes.

"And you, Paul, do *you* believe that?"

"I don't know what to believe."

"Have you ever heard machines, Paul?"

Helen broke in. "I don't *hear* them, I *feel* them. I feel them throb, throb, throbbing." She stopped abruptly, dropping her gaze again.

"But you both know that they're just the machines that give us our air and light and everything. They're buried down and down. They just go on working away like all good machines."

"Then, if machines didn't make us," said Paul, "where *did* we come from? We must have come from somewhere. Somewhere where there's trees and cats and— and other boys and girls." His shrill little voice mounted. "Why do you keep us locked away from them?"

"What?" said Em, startled. How could she begin to tell them the truth, if that was what they thought?

"Why can't we ever join them and play in the trees with them? Why do you keep the big door locked all the time?" His eyes filled with tears, but he did not cry aloud. It was that fact, that he did not cry, that decided Em more than anything else.

"I'll tell you," she said. She took one look at Jay. He nodded once, slowly. Even Jay saw there was no avoiding it this time.

The children's eyes widened. They looked at each other and back to Em.

"Before I begin," said Em, "you must promise to be brave. You will hear things you did not expect. You were each made by a mother and a father. Jay and I are only here to see that you grow up well and strong and clever. Your father and mother, Paul, and yours, Helen, are dead. Once there were twenty people here and they are all dead now."

"We know what that means," said Helen. "Not alive— like the mat and the chair. But where are they? Why aren't they here, even if they *are* dead?"

Em realized with something like relief that they had no real conception of death. Perhaps it wouldn't be so difficult, after all. That could be explained later, when it had been revealed to them why it was so important to be alive. Or would they think it important after she told them what she had to tell them?

"Because the dead have no place with the living. That is, except in their thoughts. Jay and I often think of your parents and the others with them. Don't we, Jay?"

"Eh? Oh, yes, yes."

"Because they made us, too," went on Em. "Well, not *your* actual mothers and fathers, but other clever people like them. We're grateful and happy that they made us. That's why we're happy to look after you. And that's why you must try to be as clever as they were."

The children looked puzzled.

"You mean," piped Paul, "so that we can make people like you?"

"I didn't mean that," said Em. "You will have to make others like yourselves."

"But we couldn't do that," said Helen, aghast. "We're not clever enough."

"I don't think," said Em, "that you'll need to be clever to do that when the time comes. There are other reasons for you to be clever." She rose, crossing to the big door. "Come with me," she said.

They stood looking after her for a moment, not believing their eyes. Then they rushed after her shouting excitedly.

"Em's going to take us outside."

"Can we climb the trees, Em?"

"Are there shops there?"

She turned, one metal hand on the bolt, looking down at them as they skipped about her legs.

"There aren't any trees out there. Nor shops."

They looked up at her in shocked surprise, suddenly motionless.

"Then—it *is* all lies in the books?" said Paul slowly.

"No, it's not lies. It's just that *we* haven't got them. They're in the past."

"You mean like the fairy stories? Once upon a time? All once upon a time?"

And Helen said, "There's just nothing?"

Em faced Jay as she said slowly, "I told you that you would hear things you did not expect. Are you really sure you want to go on?"

She looked from one to the other. She had expected

them to be frightened. But she'd underestimated the effect on them of living all their lives in one confined space, their wonder at being able to step out of it at last.

"Yes. Please, Em," said Helen.

"Yes, Em," said Paul. "Please."

As she slid the bolt back she had the same feeling as when the last humans had died. The feeling of inadequacy. The disquieting knowledge that when one was dealing with inanimate objects two and two made four and nothing else, but when one was dealing with humans, even little humans—*especially* little humans—the answer might be something entirely different.

She slid the door open. The dimly lit passages confronted them.

"Oh!" they cried, sounding disappointed.

"Come along," she said quickly. She took their hands. Then she saw that Jay had not come to the door with them. He hung back, awkwardly. "Aren't you coming, Jay?"

"Oh, sure, sure," he said and lumbered after them.

"No pranks, now," said Em to the children. "Keep hold of my hands."

As they walked down the corridor Helen said, "I feel it."

"I feel it, too, now," said Paul.

The slight vibration of the engines increased. They passed down a short flight of steps. "Now I *hear* it," said Helen.

"Now you see it," said Em as they turned a bend.

And there were the engines. The great engines, purring and purring, the lights winking over the panels.

"Oooh!" breathed the boy. "Look at that great wheel spinning."

"That's the one that supplies us with air," said Em.

Paul took a deep breath. "It smells funny here."

"That's ozone," Em said.

"What's ozone?"

"I'm not sure," said Em. "It's some special kind of air. It's all explained in the books. All about how to stop the machines and how to start them and how to make them go faster. You should see them when they're really going. They're only ticking over now. But, my, when they really cut loose it's wonderful."

"Why, what do they do then, Em?"

It was going right, she thought. They would understand, because now they would want to.

"Come along," she said, "and I'll show you." She led them along the walk to the control room. But there she felt doubt return. Her hand hesitated on the switch. And then, because she knew there was no turning back now, she pressed it.

The children gasped and fell back a step, stumbling, fearing they would fall. Em laid her hands upon their shoulders. "There, it's all right," she said.

The screen seemed to curve above and beneath and all around them. It was as if they were suspended in the breathing heart of the Universe. But because the children had no notion of the word *Universe*, this being the first time they had even seen the stars, to them it was like floating in a great dream, a great and wonderful dream.

It was Paul who, after many moments, broke the silence. And then he only whispered the one word, *"Stars!"* and he was not speaking to Helen or Em or Jay—or even to himself. He was addressing *them*, the stars.

"They're diamonds," said Helen. "Like in the story. Diamonds and rubies and emeralds. Reach out and get one for me, Em, so I can hold it in my hand."

"I can't," said Em. "How far away do you think they are?" realizing even as she asked it that the question could have no meaning for them.

But Helen was too excited to pursue that one. "Look," she said. "Look at that great big cloud."

In the infinitely clear depths of infinite space it *was* like a cloud. It couldn't have been anything *but* a cloud to a child who had never seen the skies of Earth. But the teacher in Em could not help saying, "That's a nebula."

But Helen did not hear her. She danced up and down, clapping her hands. "That's *my* cloud. I'm going to find a wonderful name for it. What about you, Paul? Do you want that big blue star and red star together?"

But Paul had turned away puzzledly from the screen.

"What is it, Paul?" Em asked.

"I'm just wondering," he said.

"Wondering what?"

"Why you had to keep this away from us all this time."

"Because . . ." Em faltered. "Because I didn't know whether you were ready for it."

"Ready?" he said, and though his voice asked a question, his tone held a strange confidence. "But why not?" Helen, too, turned away from the screen to look puzzled.

Heavens, thought Em, had all those precautions been unnecessary, then? She had only been carrying out instructions as best she could. And her own reasoning had told her they were wise ones. But had they been? Perhaps she and the parents alike had overestimated the dangers. Perhaps because *they* had known what it was like to have a wide world under one's feet, they had not understood that it would not be the same for children born in space. *But no*, she told herself. *They don't know all of it yet.*

And then she told them.

How this was the first starship and probably the last for a long, long time, because starships couldn't be made every day of the week to launch into space. Nor could men and women be found so easily to volunteer for the years of journeying that it entailed—the years of journeying and possibly never arriving, possibly dying before reaching their goal, but having children before they died, so that the children would carry on.

And how it had gone wrong. How they had died too soon. How the disease had struck the first generation before they were far out in interstellar space—too far out to return. How unknown radiations had produced an unknown germ that had stricken all the adults, attacking their nervous systems. How this had broken out not long before the two children had been born. And how Em helped as best she could at the births because there had been so few of the crew left by then, and those that were still alive had been stricken by the uncontrollable palsy that was the herald of death.

And then the mothers had died, and the other remnants of the crew. And they died, not quite without hope now. Not quite.

Em suddenly realized, in the middle of telling it, that talk of stars and starships could have little meaning for the children. So she digressed to explain something of what she knew of the Universe, of its vast depths and distances, of how great a venture it was to be crossing them.

She explained that this was why she and Jay had to watch over them so carefully, why she and Jay had to teach them to read and understand the books, so that they would be able to carry on the great venture. Because one day the ship would have to be piloted down to a new world. She and Jay couldn't do that unaided.

Jay told them the original purpose for which they had been brought along—to navigate the ship under the stresses of landing—and the stresses of that first takeoff from Earth. That, and to explore any worlds that might be difficult for humans to explore. But they couldn't do it without the help of humans to plan and direct.

Jay was silent. Em also waited silently. That was too much to ask of the children all at once. So they just waited.

Paul spoke first and his words seemed strangely irrelevant. He turned to Em. "Then *you* don't die— you and Jay?"

"Why, no," she answered. "We go on looking after you and then after the children you will have. We just go on and on, like all good machines." Now, she could admit the difference between them. It was better this way.

"You're not machines," said Helen stoutly. "You're too wise to be machines."

"Well, we're *wise* machines, then," Em said, and then, thinking they were getting off the subject, "so, you see, that's why there aren't any trees or cats or other children. They're too far away, like the stars."

"Which one of those stars is Earth?" said Paul. The word sounded odd on his lips.

"You can't see Earth from here," said Em. "It's much too far away. Besides, it isn't a star. It's a planet going around a star."

"Which star?" said Paul, and Em realized that she didn't know.

"I'll look it up in the charts," she said hastily, hoping

she could read them correctly, "and then I'll point it out to you. How's that?"

"Could you see all this," said Helen, "back on Earth?"

"Oh, no, never like this. Half the time you couldn't see it at all because the Sun was too bright."

Paul excitedly said, "But then it's only just a long way away. Back on Earth there's trees and cats and all those things. And—children just like us seeing them every day. Why, right now . . ."

"But there were other things," Em said quickly. "Bad things as well. Things we're free of here, thank goodness."

"What bad things?" said Helen. "Like being dizzy because of going around and around all the time?"

"No," said Em. "Nobody ever got dizzy from that. *We're* traveling at a great speed now, but we don't get dizzy, do we? No, but believe Em, there *were* bad things—lots of them." A sudden thought struck her. "Otherwise your parents and the others wouldn't have wanted to leave Earth, would they?"

"No," admitted Paul, but he didn't seem very convinced.

It was Jay—Jay who had been silent most of the time for fear of upsetting things—who said impulsively, "Don't you see? They just got tired of going around and around the same little star all the time. They didn't get giddy, they just got tired of it, sick and tired. And they didn't want that for their children.

They wanted to give them a better life, a real start in life—"

He stopped as abruptly as he had begun. He turned away as if fearing he had said the wrong thing.

Em touched his square shoulder. One look at the children's faces told her that he had said the *right* thing, the supremely right thing. Jay turned back and Em nodded, her hand still resting gratefully on his shoulder.

Paul said, "And when we get to a new world, will there be trees and cats?"

"There might be trees," said Em. "There might be cats." She had heard the humans discussing these things. "There might be—anything."

She felt a sudden pang of guilt. Was it right not to tell them the rest? She started to, then checked herself. No, the crisis had been met and surmounted. That was the important thing now.

"*Anything?*" said Paul.

"Giants, even?" said Helen, her eyes round with wonder. "Wizards? Fairy castles?"

"Yes," said Em, "there might be all of those and more. Nothing guaranteed, mind you, but anything is possible. Anything at all."

And so she did not add that it wouldn't be for another hundred and twenty years. That could be told later.

Big Sword

by Pauline Ashwell

When you're less than six inches tall, and your weapon is a thornlike sword, how can you hope to defeat invading Earthmen?

He was taller than the tallest by nearly an inch, because the pod that hatched him had hung on the Tree more than twenty days longer than the rest, kept from ripening by all the arts at the People's command. The flat spike sheathed in his left thigh was, like the rest of him, abnormally large: but it was because he represented their last defense that they gave him the name, if a thought-sign can be called that, of "Big Sword."

He was a leader from his birth, because among the People intelligence was strictly proportional to size. They had two kinds of knowledge: Tree-knowledge, which they possessed from the moment they were born; and Learned-knowledge, the slow accumulation of facts passed on from one generation to another with the perfect accuracy of transmitted thought, which again was shared by all alike. The Learned-knowledge of the People covered all the necessities that they had previously experienced: but now they were faced with a wholly new danger and they needed somebody to acquire the Learned-knowledge to deal with it. So they made use of the long-known arts that could delay ripening of the pods on the Tree. These were not used often, because neighboring pods were liable to be stunted by the growth of an extra-large one, but now there was the greatest possible need for a leader. The Big Folk, after two years of harmlessness, had suddenly revealed themselves as an acute danger, one that threatened the life of the People altogether.

Tree-knowledge Big Sword had, of course, from the moment of his hatching. The Learned-knowledge of the People was passed on to him by a succession of them sitting beside him in the tree-tops while his body swelled and hardened and absorbed the light. He would not grow any larger: the People made use of the stored energy of sunlight for their activities, but the substance of their bodies came from the Tree. For three revolutions of the planet he lay and absorbed energy and information. Then he knew all that they could pass on to him, and was ready to begin.

A week later he was sitting on the edge of a clearing in the forest, watching the Big Folk at their incomprehensible tasks. The People had studied them a little when they first appeared in the forest, and had made some attempt to get in touch with them, but without success. The Big Folk used thought all right, but chaotically: instead of an ordered succession of symbols there would come a rush of patterns and half-patterns, switching suddenly into another set altogether and then returning to the first, and at any moment the whole thing might be wiped out altogether. Those first students of the People, two generations ago, had thought that there was some connection between the disappearance of thought and the vibrating wind which the Big Folk would suddenly emit from a split in their heads. Big Sword was now certain that they were right, but the knowledge did not help him much. After the failure of their first attempts at communication the People, not being given to profitless curiosity, had left the Big Folk alone. But now a totally unexpected danger had come to light. One of the Big Folk, lumbering about the forest, had cut a branch off the Tree.

When they first arrived the Big Folk had chopped down a number of trees—ordinary trees—completely and used them for various peculiar constructions in the middle of the clearing, but that was a long time ago and the People had long since ceased to worry about it. Two generations had passed since it happened. But the attack on the Tree itself had terrified them. They had no idea why it had been made and there was no guarantee that it would not happen again. Twelve guardians had been posted round the Tree ready to do anything possible with thought or physical force to stave off another such attack, but they were no match for the Folk. The only safety lay in making contact with the Big Folk and telling them why they must leave the Tree of the People alone.

Big Sword had been watching them for two days now and his plan was almost ready. He had come to the conclusion that a large part of the difficulty lay in the fact that the Big People were hardly ever alone. They seemed to go about in groups of two or three and thought would jump from one to another at times in a confusing way: then again you would get a group whose thoughts were all completely different and reached the observer in a chaotic pattern of interference. The thing to do, he had decided, was to isolate one of them. Obviously the one to tackle would be the most intelligent of the group, the leader, and it was clear which one filled that position: he stood out among his companions as plainly as Big Sword. There were one or two factors to be considered further, but that evening, Big Sword had decided, he would be ready to act.

Meanwhile the Second Lambdan Exploratory Party had troubles of their own. Mostly these were the professional bothers that always accompany scientific expeditions; damaged equipment, interesting sidelines for which neither equipment nor workers happened to be available, not enough hours in the day. Apart from that there was the constant nag of the gravitation,

twenty per cent higher than that of Earth, and the
effect, depressing until you got used to it, of the mono-
chromatic scenery, laid out in darker and lighter shades
of black and gray. Only the red soil and red rocks
varied that monotony, with an effect which to Terrestrial eyes was somewhat sinister. Nevertheless, the
Expedition were having fewer troubles than they expected. Lambda, apparently, was a thoroughly safe
planet. Whatever those gray-and-black jungles might
look like, it appeared that they had nothing harmful
in them.

At thirty light-years away from Earth most personal
troubles had got left behind. John James Jordan, however, the leader of the party, had brought his with
him. His most urgent responsibility was in the next
cabin, in bed and, it was to be hoped, asleep.

There was no doubt about it, a man who made his
career in space had no business to get married. Some
men, of course, could take their wives with them: there
were three married couples on the expedition, though
they were with the first party at base on the coast.
But for a spaceman to marry a woman and leave her
at home didn't make sense.

He wondered, now, what he had thought he was
doing. Marriage had been a part of that hectic interval
between his first expedition and his second, when he
had arrived home to find that space exploration was
News and everybody wanted to know him. He had
been just slightly homesick, that first time. The idea

of having somebody to come back to had been attractive.

The actual coming back, three years later, had not been so good. He had had time to realize that he scarcely knew Cora. Most of their married life seemed to have been spent at parties: he would arrive late, after working overtime, and find Cora already in the thick of it. He was going to have more responsibility preparing for the third expedition: he was going to have to spend most of his time on it. He wondered how Cora was going to take it. She had never complained when he wasn't there, during the brief period of their married life: but somehow what he remembered wasn't reassuring.

Just the same, it was a shock to find that she had divorced him a year after his departure—one of the first of the so-called "space divorces." It was a worse shock, though, to find that he now had a two-year-old son.

The rule in a space divorce was that the divorced man had the right to claim custody of his children, providing that he could make adequate arrangements for them during his absence. That would have meant sending Ricky to some all-year-round school. There was no sense to that. Cora's new husband was fond of him. Jordan agreed to leave Ricky with his mother. He even agreed, three years later on his next leave, not to see Ricky—Cora said that someone had told the little boy that her husband was not his real father and contact with somebody else claiming that position was likely to upset him.

Once or twice during his Earth-leaves—usually so crammed with duties that they made full-time exploration look like a holiday—Jordan got news of Cora. Apparently she was a rising star in the social world. He realized gradually, that she had married him because for a brief time he had been News, and could take her where she wanted to be. He was vaguely relieved that she had got something out of their marriage: it was nice that somebody did. He was prepared to grant her doings the respect due to the incomprehensible. Nevertheless he was worried, for a moment, when he heard that she had been divorced yet again and remarried—to a prominent industrialist this time. He wondered how Ricky had taken it.

His first actual contact with Cora in about seven years came in the form of a request from her lawyer that he should put his signature to an application for entrance to a school. Merely a formality. The insistence on that point roused his suspicions and he made some inquiries about the school in question.

Half an hour after getting answers he had found Cora's present address, booked a passage on the Transequatorial Flight and canceled his engagements for the next twenty-four hours.

He was just in time to get aboard the flier. He had taken a bundle of urgent papers with him and he had three hours of flight in which to study them, but he

hardly tried to do so. His conscience felt like a Lo-
thornian cactus-bird trying to break out of the egg.

Why on Earth, why in Space, why in the Universe
hadn't he taken some sort of care of his son?

He had never visited Antarctica City before and he
found it depressing. With great ingenuity somebody
had excavated a building-space in the eternal ice and
filled it with a city which was an exact copy of all the
other cities. He wondered why anybody had thought
it worthwhile.

Cora's house seemed less a house than an animated
set for a stereo on The Life of the Wealthy Classes.
It had been decorated in the very latest style—he
recognized one of two motifs which had been suggested
by the finds of the First Lambdan Expedition, mingled
with the usual transparent furniture and electrified
drapes. He was contemplating a curious decorative
motif, composed of a hooked object which he recognized vaguely as some primitive agricultural imple-
ment and what looked like a pileman's drudge—but of
course that particular mallet-shape had passed through
innumerable uses—when Cora came in.

Her welcome was technically perfect: it combined a
warm greeting with just a faint suggestion that it was
still open to her to have him thrown out by the mech-
man if it seemed like a good idea. He decided to get
the business over as soon as possible.

"What's the matter with Ricky, Cora? Why do you
want to get rid of him?"

Cora's sparkle-crusted brows rose delicately.

"Why, Threejay, what a thing to say."

The idiotic nickname, almost forgotten, caught him off balance for a moment, but he knew exactly what he wanted to say.

"This school you want to send him to is for maladjusted children. It takes complete responsibility, replacing parents—you wouldn't be allowed to see him for the next three years at least."

"It's a very fine school, Threejay. Camillo insisted we should send him to the best one available."

Camillo must be the new husband.

"Why?" repeated Jordan.

The welcome had drained right out of Cora's manner. "May I ask why this sudden uprush of parental feeling? You've never shown any interest in Ricky before. You've left him to me. I'm not asking you to take any responsibility. I'm just asking you to sign that form."

"Why?"

"Because he's unbearable! Because I won't have him in the house! He pries round—there's no privacy. He finds out everything and then uses it to make trouble. He's insulted half our friends. Camillo won't have him in the house and neither will I. If you don't want him to go to that school, perhaps you'll suggest an alternative."

Jordan was shaken, but tried not to show it. "I'd like to see him, Cora."

As swiftly as it had arisen Cora's rage sank out of sight. "Of course you can see him, Threejay!" She turned to the wall-speaker and murmured briefly into it. "Who knows, maybe the sight of a really, true father is all he needs! You can just have a nice fatherly chat with him before you have to catch your flier back, and then he'll settle down and turn into a model citizen."

The door slid open and a boy came quietly in. He was a very neat and tidy boy, small for his age, with a serious, almost sad expression. He said gently, "Good morning, Cora."

Cora spoke over her shoulder. "Ricky, dear, who do you think this is?"

Ricky looked at the visitor and his eyes widened.

"You . . . you're Dr. Jordan, aren't you? You wrote that book about Cranil—it's called 'The Fossil Planet.' And I saw you on the stereo two nights ago. You were talking about that place where all the forests are gray and black. And—" Ricky stopped with his mouth half open. His face went blank.

"That's who I am," said Jordan gravely.

"I know," Ricky swallowed. "But you're here . . . I mean . . . this sounds silly, but I suppose . . . I mean, you wouldn't be my father, would you?"

"Don't put on an act, Ricky," said Cora harshly. "You know perfectly well he's your father."

Ricky turned rather white. He shook his head. "No, honestly. I knew my father's name was Jordan, but I just didn't connect it up. I say—" he stopped short.

"Yes, Ricky?"

"I suppose you wouldn't have time to talk to me a little? About Lambda, I mean. Because I really am interested—not just kid stuff. I want to be a xeno-biologist."

Cora laughed, a delicate metallic sound.

"Why be so modest, Ricky? After all, he's your father. He's apparently decided it's time he took an interest in you. He's due back to that place that fascinates you so much in a week or two, so I don't see how he'll do that unless he takes you with him. Why not ask him to?"

Ricky went scarlet and then very pale. He looked quickly away, but not before Jordan had had time to see the eager interest in his face replaced by sick resignation.

"Why shouldn't you take him, Threejay?" went on Cora. "These Mass-Time ships have lots of room. You've decided that it's time you were responsible for him instead of me. Those books he reads are full of boys who made good in space. Why don't you—"

"Yes, why don't I?" said Jordan abruptly.

"Don't!" said Ricky sharply. "Please, don't! Honestly, I know it's a joke . . . I mean I don't read that kid stuff now . . . but—"

"No joke," said Jordan. "As Cora says, there's lots of room. Do you want to come?"

And I'd had my psycho check only the week before, reflected Jordan, and they didn't find a thing.

*   *   *

He noticed suddenly that a report was moving through the scanner on his desk—the latest installment of Woodman's researches on the sexual cycles of Lambdan freshwater organisms. He'd intended to read that tonight instead of mulling over all this stuff about Ricky.

He pushed the switch back to the beginning, but it was no use. He remembered how he had felt—how Cora's needling had made him feel—and how Ricky had looked when he grasped that the proposal was serious. No chance at all of backing out then—not that he had wanted to. It was true that, with Mass-Time flight, there was plenty of room; one feature of the drive was that within certain limits the bigger the ship the faster it would go. And he had complete authority over the selection of personnel for this second expedition, which was to reinforce the team already settled on Lambda. Ricky's inclusion was taken with a surprising lack of concern by the rest of the staff. And it had looked as though his insane action was working out all right. Until the last two days Ricky had been no trouble at all.

If anything, Ricky had been too desperately anxious to keep out of the way and avoid being a nuisance, but he had seemed completely happy. Jordan's project of getting to know him had never got very far, because his time was fully occupied, but Ricky had spent the weeks before blast-off mainly in the Inter-stellar Institute, chaperoned by young Woodman, who had taken a fancy to him. Jordan had taken time out once or twice during that period to worry over the fact that he was hardly seeing the boy, but once they got aboard ship it would be different.

Once aboard ship, absorbed in checking stores and setting up projects to go into operation as soon as they landed, it wasn't—once the party's settled and working, it'll be different. He'd have some time to spare.

Unfortunately that hadn't been soon enough. He should have paid some attention to Cora. She wouldn't have got worked up like that over nothing. She had said Ricky made trouble. He'd done that all right. And Jordan had known nothing about it till it attained the dimensions of a full-blown row.

Rivalry on the expedition was usually friendly enough. Unfortunately Cartwright and Penn, the two geologists, didn't get on. They had different methods of working and each was suspicious of the value of the other's work. But without Ricky they wouldn't have come to blows on it.

Quite accidentally the riot had been started by Ellen Scott. As soil specialist she had an interest in geology. Talking to Cartwright she had happened to say something about the date of the Great Rift. Cartwright had shot out of his chair.

"Ellen—where did you get that idea? Who told it to you?"

Ellen looked surprised.

"I thought you did, Peter. The Great Rift's your pet

subject. If you didn't, I suppose it was Penn."

"I haven't mentioned it to anyone. I only worked it out a couple of days ago. It's in my notes now, on my desk. Penn must have been going through them. Where is he?"

"Calm down, Peter!" Ellen got to her feet in astonishment. "Probably he worked it out too—you may have mentioned something that set him on the track. He must have mentioned it to me in the last few days, I think . . . that is, if he was the one who told me." She looked puzzled. "I don't remember discussing it with him. No, I believe—" she broke off suddenly and refused to say any more. Cartwright, unmollified, strode off to look for Penn. Dr. Scott departed in search of Ricky.

"Ricky, do you remember a day or two ago we were talking about the Great Rift?"

Ricky looked up from the microscope he was using.

"Sure," he said. "Why?" His smile faded and he began to look worried. "What's happened?"

"You remember you said something about the date— that it was about fifteen thousand years ago? You did say that, didn't you?"

Ricky's expression had faded to a watchful blank, but he nodded.

"Well, who told you that? How did you know?"

"Somebody said it," said Ricky flatly. He did not sound as though he expected to be believed.

Ellen Scott frowned.

"Listen, Ricky. Dr. Cartwright's got the idea that somebody must have looked through the papers on his desk and read that date. He says he didn't mention it to anyone. There may be trouble. If you did get curious and took a look at his notes—well, now is the time to say so. It's not a good thing to have done, of course, but nobody'll pay much attention once it's cleared up."

"I didn't look," said Ricky wretchedly. "I don't remember how I knew, but I didn't look. Honestly not."

Unfortunately by that time Cartwright and Penn had already started arguing which ended with both of them crashing through the wall of the dining cabin— which had not been built to take assaults of that kind— and throwing Barney the cook into a kind of hysterics. After that Jordan came on the scene.

Ricky had come and told him about it all. At least, he'd said that he had somehow learned that the date of the Great Rift had been fixed, and had mentioned it to Dr. Scott while they were talking about geology. He didn't know how he had learned it. He denied looking through Cartwright's papers.

It was something that he had told the story, but then he must have thought that Ellen Scott would if he didn't.

Jordan's thoughts wandered off to Ellen for a moment. She was another person who believed that people who chose to work on alien planets must avoid personal ties. How right she was.

Nothing more had happened. Cartwright and Penn seemed to be on somewhat better terms, having purged their animosity. But Ricky had been going round with a haunted and hopeless look on his face and Jordan was going crazy trying to think up an approach to the matter which would not drive the boy still further away from him. But if he really made a habit of prying into private papers—and Cora had accused him of just that, after all—something must be done about it.

But what?

Jordan sighed, turned the viewer back to the beginning again and started to concentrate on Woodman's report. He had read three frames when the silence was split by a terrified bellow from the direction of the forest.

"Uelph! Uelph! Dewils. Uelph!"

Jordan shot through the door, grabbing a flashlight on the way. It was hardly needed: three moons were in the sky and their combined light was quite enough to show him the huge shape blundering among the cabins.

"Barney!" he shouted. "Stand still! What's the matter?"

Barney—seventeen stone on Earth, over twenty on Lambda—came to a halt and blinked at the flashlight. He put up a huge hand, feeling at his face. He seemed to be wearing some sort of mask or muffler over his mouth—otherwise he was draped in flannelette pajamas of brilliant hue and was barefooted. He ripped off the muffler—whatever it was—and threw it away. His utterance was a little clearer, but not much.

"Dewils in a voresh. Caught eee. Woot ticky tuff on a wouth."

He was gasping and sweating and Jordan was seriously worried. Barney was a superb cook, but he was apt to get excited and the extra gravitation of Lambda produced a slight strain on his heart. At that moment Ricky appeared like a silent shadow at his father's elbow.

"What's the matter with him?" As usual the boy looked neat and alert, although at the moment he was wearing pajamas and a robe. Jordan gestured toward his cabin.

"Take Barney in there and see what's sticking his mouth up." Several other people had appeared by this time, including Ellen Scott in a brilliant robe and Woodman in rumpled pajamas. Jordan sent Ellen to switch on the overhead floods and organized a search party.

Half an hour later Barney's mouth had been washed free from the gummy material which had been sticking his lips together and he was in some shape to explain.

"I woke up suddenly lying out in the forest. All damp it was." He groaned faintly. "I can feel my lumbago coming on already. I was lyin' flat on my back and there was somethin' over my arms—rope or somethin'. My mouth was all plastered up and there was a thing sittin' on my chest. I got a glimpse of it out of the crack of me eyes, and then it went. There was more of them round. They was shoutin'."

"Shouting?" repeated Jordan. "You mean just making a noise?"

"No, sir, they was shouting in English. I couldn't hear what, but it was in words all right. They said 'People.' That was the only word I got, but that's it right enough. 'People.' Then I got my arms free and started to swipe around. I got hold of one of them and it stung me and I let it go."

He pointed to a neat puncture wound in the flesh at the base of his thumb. Jordan got out antiseptics and bathed it.

"I got up and ran back," Barney went on. "I was only a little way into the forest—I could still see the lights here. I ran as hard as I could but me feet kept slippin'." The light of remembered panic was in his eyes. "They stuck somethin' over me mouth—I couldn't breathe. It took me hours to get it off. I dunno what it was."

"It was a leaf," said Woodman. He produced a large leaf, perhaps twenty inches long: it was dark gray and one surface was smeared with a dully shining substance. "It's been coated with some kind of vegetable gum."

"But how did you get into the forest, Barney?" demanded Dr. Scott.

Barney shook his head miserably.

"He walked," said another of the party. "On his own.

Tracks of his feet in the mud. You've been sleep-walking, Barney."

"Then where did he get the gag?" demanded Wood-man. "This gum comes from a plant which is quite rare and there aren't any within a hundred yards of the clearing. Besides, we found the place where he'd been lying. A couple of saplings were bent over and the ends shoved in the mud—those were used to hold his arms down, I reckon. No, he was attacked all right, but what did it?"

"I suppose," said Dr. Scott slowly, "this couldn't have been somebody's idea of a joke?"

There was a brief silence. Ricky looked up suddenly and caught his father's eye. His face went rigid, but he said nothing.

"We shall have to assume it wasn't," said Jordan. "That means precautions. We always assumed that Lambda was a safe planet. Apparently we were wrong. Until we know what happened no one goes out alone. Those of you who have observations to make outside will have to work in pairs and with your radios turned on. We'll arrange for a monitor on all the individual frequencies. The floods had better stay on tonight and we'll have a patrol—three men keeping in touch. Two hours for each of us. Doc, will you see to Barney?"

The medical officer nodded and took Barney off to his cabin, and its specially strengthened bunk. Jordan looked thoughtfully at his son.

"You'd better get back to bed, Ricky. Unless you have anything to contribute."

Ricky was standing stiffly upright. "I haven't," he said.

"Get along, then. Now about this patrol—"

Jordan put himself on the first shift of the patrol—he wouldn't be able to sleep. Why in Space had he brought Ricky? Either he had brought him into danger or—worse—Ricky was somehow at the bottom of this. He spent a good deal of time running errands for Barney. He had not seemed to mind it, but how did you tell what a boy was thinking? Might he have thought it funny to send big Barney lumbering in panic through the forest? And how could he have done it?

Jordan remembered that Ricky had once been found reading the article on hypnosis in the Terrestrial Encyclopedia.

And if Ricky was innocent, what could be at the bottom of that ludicrous and inefficient attack?

In the top of the tallest tree, Big Sword waited for daylight and brooded over the failure of his plan.

It was easy enough to get the biggest of the Big Folk into the forest. He had discovered that for part of the time they lay folded out flat in their enclosures, with their eyes shut, and during this time they were more sensitive to suggestion than when they were active. Big Sword, whose own eyes had an internal shutter, found eyelids rather fascinating: he had been tempted to experiment with Barney's but had refrained. He thought bitterly that he might as well have done so.

He had summoned twelve of the People and all of them thinking together had got the Big Person to its feet and walking. It had occurred to Big Sword that the receptiveness of the Big Person might be improved if they got it to lie down again. He had further decided that in view of the blanking-out of thought when the creatures began to blow through their face-split, this aperture had better be shut.

That, he now knew, had been a mistake. No sooner was the gummed leaf in place on the Big Person's face than its eyes had popped open and showed every sign of coming right out of its face. There had been just warning enough in its thoughts for the band of People to hop out of range, except for Big Sword, who had had to use his pike for the first time in his life, to get free. Then the great arms had swung dangerously about and the creature had thrashed to its feet. After that there was no hope of making contact. Its mind was in a turmoil, making the People actively uncomfortable: they had retreated as far as they could, until the interwoven lives of trees and other forest creatures were sufficiently interposed to reduce the Big Person's thought to a comfortable intensity.

Big Sword had been surprised by the low level of intelligence shown by the Big Person. It had made no effort at all to understand him—its thoughts were a much worse muddle than any of the others he had investigated. Perhaps he had made a mistake? Perhaps size among these monsters was not directly connected

with intelligence? Or perhaps it was an inverse relationship?

Big Sword was suddenly desperately thirsty and
tired. He slid into the rain-filled cup of an enormous
leaf—to soak up water through the million mouths of
his skin and make his plans afresh.

The camp next morning was subdued and rather
weary. Nobody had got their full sleep. Now there
was all the awkward business of rearranging a full-
time research program so that nobody should have to
go into the forest alone. The lurking menace which last
night had provided a formidable thrill, this morning
was nothing more than a vague, dreary uneasiness.
Furthermore there was always the possibility that it
would turn out to be nothing more than the work of
an ingenious kid with a distorted sense of humor. And
nobody liked to think what that would do to Jordan.

The working parties dispersed. Those whose work
took them to the laboratory sheds tried to concentrate
on it. Ricky, who had decided that this was not a
morning for wrestling with lessons, slipped off to see
if Barney wanted any odd jobs done, and was sent to
pick fresh beans in the hydroponics shed.

The mechanical job helped to keep his mind steady.
Having once got out of a nightmare, it was creeping
round him again. This time with a difference.

There had got to be an explanation somewhere.

When he had left the house in Antarctica he had

seemed to leave all his troubles behind. No more need to keep a continual watch on himself, in case he let something out. No more temptation, when in spite of himself he had put his foot in it again, to come out with something really startling and see what they could do about it. He was free. He had been free for months.

Then it started happening all over again. He had heard all sorts of scientific gossip—people here talked shop all the time. How was he to know what he'd heard and what he didn't? How could he stop this happening again, now that whatever it was had followed him out here?

There was just one ray of hope. He couldn't possibly have had anything to do with what happened to Barney. If he could only find out what did that, some real solid explanation he could show everybody, then he might somehow be able to tell someone of the way he seemed to pick up knowledge without noticing it, knowledge he had no right to have—

Anyway, doing something was better than just sitting and waiting for things to go wrong again.

He delivered the beans to the kitchen and wandered out. The raw, red earth of the clearing shone like paint in the sun. In places he could still see the traces of Barney's big feet, going and coming, leading into the forest. There, among the black leaves and blacker shadows, lurked some real, genuine, tangible menace you could go for with a stick. There was a good supply of sticks stacked by his father's cabin for the benefit of the working parties. Ricky provided himself with one.

Big Sword had finished drinking—or bathing, whichever way you looked at it—and had climbed out of the diminished pool in the leaf-cup to spread his membranes in the sun. He looked like a big bat, lying spread out on the leaf. The black webs that stretched between his arms and legs and his sides would snap back into narrow rolls when he wanted to move, but when he extended them to catch the sunlight they covered a couple of square feet. They absorbed all the light in the visible range and well into the ultra-violet and infra-red. Like most organisms on Lambda, Big Sword supported himself by a very efficient photo-synthesis.

He had only just begun to make up for the wear and tear of the night—continuous activity in the dark was exhausting—when he felt the call out of the forest.

"Longfoot is going, Big Sword. Longfoot is going on the Journey. You wished to see. Come quickly!"

Big Sword's membranes snapped into thin ridges along his arms and legs and he bounded off among the trees. The Long Journey was mysterious to him, as it was to all of the People before the urge actually came to them—but the rest were content to leave it as a mystery. Big Sword wanted to know more.

He came in flying leaps to the edge of the forest

where the trees stopped short on the edge of the Great Rift. Some twenty or so of the People were gathered on the edge of the sheer cliff. Longfoot sat among them, his legs twitching occasionally with the urge to be off. As Big Sword arrived Longfoot shot to his feet, eager to depart.

"Where are you going?" demanded Big Sword. "What will you find over there, Longfoot? Why do you want to cross the waste, with no water and no shade? You will be dried to a stick before you get halfway across."

But Longfoot's mind was shut off; he had no longer any interest in Big Sword, or the People, or the danger to the Tree. He did not know why he had to go down on to the waste of boulders and small stones, but the urge could no longer be resisted. He dropped over the edge of the cliff, bouncing from ledge to ledge until he reached the bottom, and set off across the wide, rock-strewn plain, along the lines of shadow cast by the newly risen sun.

Big Sword watched him sadly. He himself was nearly a year away from feeling that call which had come to Longfoot, and the thought of his own journeying did not trouble him yet. He had been warned early of the dangers of going out on to the waste and, with the habit of logical thought strongly cultivated in him, he was troubled about what would happen. The waste stretched almost as far as he could see—at least twelve miles. At the end of it was the dark line which might have been a far-off continuation of the forest. But why

Longfoot should have wished to go there, or the many thousands of the People who had made that journey before him, Big Sword could not see.

He went back into the forest and found another perch on the edge of the clearing. Few of the Big People were in sight. He was conscious of vague alarms emanating from those who were within reach—it was an emotion foreign to his experience, but he disliked it. He wondered how to set about detaching a specimen from the group, since the direct method had proved unsuitable.

He became suddenly and sharply aware that one had detached itself already and was coming slowly toward him.

Ricky had seen the little black figure sail out of the shadows and land on an equally black leaf. It took all his concentration to make it out when it had stopped moving, but he at last managed to fix its position. Slowly, casually, he wandered toward it, observing it out of the corner of his eye.

Its body was a blob perhaps four inches long and its head about half of that, joined on by a short neck. It rested on its bent forelimbs and the hind legs stuck up like those of a grasshopper; they looked to be at least twice as long as trunk and head together. As he sidled closer, Ricky could make out the big convex eyes, gray with black slitlike pupils, filling more than half the face. Ricky knew the fauna list of Lambda by heart; this creature was not on it. It must be one of Barney's "little devils" all right.

The creature sat quietly on its big leaf as he approached, with no sign of having noticed him. Now it was just within his reach if he stretched up. One more step and he would be right under it—ahhhh!

He had only begun to grab when Big Sword bounced over his head, landed lightly on the ground behind him and leaped sideways into another tree.

Ricky turned, slowly, and began his careful stalk again. He was murmuring softly to himself, coaxing words derived from rabbit and guinea-pig owners of his acquaintance: "Come on, come on! Come to uncle. He won't hurt you. Nothing to be afraid of. Come on, you little brute. Come—"

Big Sword sailed away from his grasping hand to land on a branch ten feet farther into the forest.

Ricky had entirely forgotten the prohibition on leaving the clearing; he had forgotten everything except the desire to get hold of this creature, to have it close enough to examine, to hold it gently in his hand and get it tame. His stick lay forgotten on the earth outside the forest.

Big Sword was getting irritated and slightly flustered. It was easy enough to avoid getting caught, but he didn't wish to play tag with this creature, he wanted to tame it, to make it understand him. And its mind seemed to be shut. What was more, every so often it would begin that infuriating blowing process which seemed to drain away its thoughts out of his reach. To know when it was going to grab he had to watch it the whole time. Finally he took refuge on a branch ten feet above its head and sat down to consider.

Ricky, at the bottom of the tree, was experiencing all the emotions of a dog which has treed a squirrel and now has to persuade it to come within reach. Apparently he was licked. If only the little beast would drop on to that branch there—where that applelike object was—and begin to eat it, perhaps, so that it could forget he was there . . .

Suddenly, the little brute did. At least it dropped to the lower branch and put its long-fingered hands on the round knob. Ricky's mouth opened in amazement.

His hands itched, but he kept them firmly at his sides. Perhaps he had been standing there so long it had forgotten about him and thought he was part of the landscape. Perhaps if he spread his arms out very, very slowly it would take them for branches and—

Something like a small explosion happened inside his head. He blinked and gasped, forgetting all about immobility. He froze again hastily, expecting the creature to be out of sight. But it was still there.

Big Sword observed this reaction to his vehement negative with stirrings of hope. The idea of doing what this creature wanted, as a means of starting communication by demonstration, had seemed a singularly forlorn one. But the Big Creature had clearly noticed *something*.

Big Sword decided that it was time to try a suggestion of his own. He thought—hard—on the proposition that the Big Creature should turn around and look the other way.

The Big Creature ducked its head and blinked its eyes again. Big Sword got the impression that these reactions were caused by the strength of his thought. He tried again, gently.

Something was getting through. Weakly, faintly he felt a negative reply. The Big Creature refused to turn its back.

Big Sword put out another suggestion. Let the Big Creature take one step sideways, away from him.

Hesitantly, the Big Person did. Big Sword copied its direction in a joyful leap and ended on a level with the creature's head.

The next thought reached him, fuzzy but comprehensible. "If you understand me, put your hands on top of your head."

Watching suspiciously for any sudden move, Big Sword obeyed. The posture was not one he could keep up for long without losing his balance, but he felt the sudden surge of excitement in the Big Creature and was encouraged.

"Now watch! I shall sit down on the ground. Do you understand what that means? I'm going to sit down."

The Big Creature folded up in an awkward way; its knees were on the wrong side of its body, but Big

Sword recognized the operation. He followed it with a thought of his own.

"I will spread my membranes out."

The Big Creature's astonishment was a dazzling shock and he put out a protest. In reply came something which could be an apology. He sharpened his thoughts and put out the next one with all the clearness at his command.

"We have proved that we can make contact. Now we have to practice thinking to and fro until we understand clearly."

He had just felt the other's incoherent agreement when the interruption began. Another of the Big Creatures came lumbering between the trees.

"Ricky! Scatter my stuffing, what are you doing here? You'll be in the doghouse for sure. Do you want Barney's little black devils to carry you away?"

Ricky scrambled to his feet in alarm.

"Sorry, Dr. Woodman, I forgot. I was . . . looking at things and I came in here without thinking. I'm awfully sorry."

"No harm done. Come out before we have any more alarms and excursions."

Big Sword felt an impulse of despair from the Big Creature which he had at last succeeded in taming; it seemed to regret this interruption even more than he did. It was anxious that the second Big Creature should not see him, so he remained still, one dark shape among many and effectively invisible; but he sent a thought after the tame one: "Come again! I will be on the edge of the clearing. Come again!" and was nearly knocked over by the energy of its reply.

Woodman marched Ricky firmly out of the forest.

"Now you're here you may as well be useful. I want to go up to my pet pool and I can't find a chaperone. If I've timed it rightly, we should find something interesting up there."

Ricky summoned up a show of polite interest. Normally he would have been delighted.

"Is it the pseudohydras again?"

"That's right. Remember when we saw them catching those things like two-tailed torpedoes?"

"Yes, but you said all the ones in the pool had been eaten now."

"They have. Here we are. Don't lean over like that— they won't like your shadow. Lie down. So!"

Ricky lay on his belly and stared down into the transparent water. Except where it was shadowed it reflected the brilliant blue of the sky; the only thing on Lambda that had a familiar color. He felt, suddenly, stirrings of homesickness, but they vanished quickly. Homesick, when the most wonderful thing possible had just happened? Nonsense!

He concentrated on the pseudohydras. They lived just where the pool overflowed into a small brown stream. Each consisted mainly of a network of branching white threads, up to six inches long, issuing from a small blobby body anchored on the stones. There were perhaps fifty of them, and together their tentacles made a net across the mouth of the stream which nothing larger than a wheat-grain could escape. The sluggish waters of the stream must all pass through this living mesh, carrying anything unlucky enough to swim out of the pool; the tentacles were immensely sticky and could hold struggling creatures several times the size of the pseudohydra's own body, until the flesh of the tentacles had flowed slowly around them and enclosed them in a capsule whose walls slowly digested them away.

"See there?" whispered Woodman.

Here and there one of the tentacles ended in a transparent, hard-edged blob. Small dark cigar-shaped objects jerked uneasily within it, perhaps a dozen in each little case.

"It's caught some more torpedoes!" whispered Ricky. "Little tiny ones this time."

"Not caught," answered Woodman. "I thought they'd be ripe today! Watch that one—it's nearly ready to split."

A few minutes later the capsule indicated did split. The tiny torpedo shapes, three or four millimeters long, spilled out into the water. They hovered uncertainly, veering here and there under the uneven propulsion of the water-jets emerging from the two-pronged hind end. Ricky gasped.

"It's let them go! And look—there's one rubbing

against a tentacle and not getting caught. What's happened?"

Two of the little torpedo shapes came together. They jerked uncertainly round each other, then swiveled to lie parallel. They moved off together.

Others were paired already. One pair separated as Ricky watched them. The two little torpedoes shot off crazily. One came right under his eyes and he saw that it was emitting a faint milky stream.

Woodman's hand came down, holding a pipette. The torpedo veered off. Woodman sucked up a drop of water and held out the pipette.

"There," he said softly. Tiny specks, barely visible, floated in the drop.

"Eggs," said Woodman.

"Eggs! But—these are babies. The other ones were much bigger."

"So they were, Ricky. Do you know what these are going to hatch into? More torpedoes? Not on your life! Unless there's something else crazy about the life cycle, these will hatch into little pseudohydras."

Ricky rolled over to stare at him. "But what are the big torpedoes, then?"

"This is how I see it. You know about the reproductive cycles in Coelenterates, back on Earth? Especially hydroids like Obelia and so on? The sessile ones reproduce by budding for a while. Then they start to produce buds which don't turn out like the parents. Those break off and go swimming away on their own.

They feed and get big and in the end they produce eggs or sperm, and the fertilized eggs produce a new sessile generation. Well, here the free-living forms—the torpedoes—are ready to lay eggs as soon as they're released. They mate a few minutes after hatching and lay eggs as soon as they're fertilized. But after that they aren't finished. They go swimming around the pool and feed and get fat. And when they're full grown, they come swimming back to the old pseudohydras, and the pseudohydras eat them and use the food to produce a whole new crop of little torpedoes. Get it?"

Ricky scowled. "What a disgusting animal."

"Nonsense! It's a beautiful piece of natural economy. Don't be a snob, Ricky. Just because no terrestrial organism evolved this way you think it's unethical. Some Earth creatures beat pseudohydra hollow for nastiness—think of some of the parasites. Think of the barnacles, degenerate male parasitic on the female. There just aren't any ethics in evolution except that the species shall survive, if you call that an ethic."

Ricky looked at him doubtfully. "We've evolved. And we bother about other species, too."

Woodman nodded. "We try to—some of us. But our survival has meant that a good many other species didn't."

Something else occurred to Ricky. "This sort of whatsit—alternate generations—has evolved lots of times on Earth, hasn't it?"

"Sure. Dozens of different lines evolved it independently, not to mention all the Lambdan forms that have it, and a few on Arcturus III, and some on Roche's—it's one of the basic dodges, apparently. One stage makes the most of the status quo and the other acts as an insurance against possible changes. Once a well-balanced set of hereditary characters has appeared it can repeat itself fast by asexual reproduction, without the disorganization of chromosome reassortment and so on. On the other hand, should conditions change, sexually produced population has a much better chance of showing up a few adaptable forms. Some lines of life have dropped the sexual stage, just as some have dropped the asexual, but it probably doesn't pay in the long run."

"How does a stage get dropped?"

Woodman considered. "I suppose the first stage might go like this: one single asexual stage—one of these pseudohydras, for instance—happens to get isolated. Say all the rest in the pool die off. It can produce its little torpedoes, but there are no mates for them. The pseudohydra goes on reproducing asexually—you've seen how they split down the middle—and in the end a mutant form occurs which doesn't waste its substance producing useless torpedoes and that breeds faster than the others and in the end replaces them. That's just one way it could happen. In one of the African lakes there used to be annual swarms of jellyfish, all male. One single asexual stage must have got trapped in that lake, God knows how long ago, and

it went on producing those useless male jellyfish century after century, while asexual reproduction kept
the species going."

"What happened to it?"

Woodman scowled. "Silly fools polluted the lake with
industrial waste and the jellyfish died out. Come on,
it's time for lunch."

Ellen Scott put away the last of her soil samples and
scowled thoughtfully at her apparatus. Tensions in the
camp were mounting and everyone was snapping at
everybody else. One party had decided that Barney's
adventure was somehow due to Ricky, and wanted to
call off the precautions that hindered their work. The
other stuck to it that Ricky could not have organized
it and that precautions were still necessary. Anyway,
who in the other party was prepared to tell Doc that
there was no danger in the forest except for his son?

Ellen told herself that she was neutral. She didn't
know whether or not Ricky was behind their troubles
and didn't much care, if only he would leave off tearing
his father's nerves to pieces. She had heard a little
gossip about him on Earth after it had been announced
that he was to join the expedition, and though she had
discounted it at the time, after the business of Cartwright's report she was inclined to believe it.

People whose work lay in space had no business with
marriage and children. She had decided that for herself
years ago. You could run planetary research properly,

or you could run a family properly. Not both. Children were part of life on Earth; the settled pattern of security, with which she had grown so bored, was necessary to them. When they were older, perhaps—Ricky had seemed perfectly happy at first.

But what on Lambda was the matter with him now? He'd been going around in a dream ever since the night of Barney's adventure. Starting suddenly to talk to himself, breaking off with equal suddenness and an air of annoyance. He didn't seem now to be particularly worried by the suspicions floating around the camp, although he seemed the sort of sensitive boy to be desperately upset by them. In fact over that affair with Cartwright he had been upset, and this affair was worse.

And Jordan was obviously heading for a nervous breakdown if this went on much longer.

Ricky, lying in his cabin and theoretically taking his afternoon rest—imposed because of Lambda's longer day—had come to the conclusion that it was time to tell father about his Research. Despite his absorption in his overwhelming new interest, he was vaguely aware that the grown-ups were getting bothered. For another he could now "talk" fluently with Big Sword and haltingly with the rest of the People; he knew what they wanted and there was no excuse for delaying any longer. Besides, the results of Research were not meant to be kept to oneself, they were meant to be free to everyone.

He allowed himself to think for a moment about the possibilities of his newly discovered power. Of course, people had been messing about with telepathy for centuries, but they had never got anywhere much. Perhaps only a fully developed telepath, coming of a race to which telepathy was the sole method of communication, could teach a human being how to control and strengthen his wayward and uncertain powers. Or perhaps, thought Ricky, the people who were really capable of learning the trick got into so much trouble before they could control it that they all simply shut it off as hard as they could, so that the only ones who tried to develop it were those in whom it never became strong enough to do anything useful. He himself had now, at last, learned how to shut off his awareness of other minds; it was the first necessity for clear reception that one should be able to deafen oneself to all minds except one. It occurred to him that he'd better make that point clear straight off: that he was not going to eavesdrop on anyone else's thoughts. Never again.

But obviously the thing had terrific potentialities for research, not only into the difficult and thorny problem of the connection between mind and matter, or into contact with alien races. Why, he could probably find out what really went on in the minds of terrestrial animals, those that had minds; and he could find out what it was that people experienced in a Mass-Time field, which they could never

properly remember afterwards, and—oh, all sorts
of things!

Ricky got up from his bunk. His father ought to be
free at this moment; it was the one time of day he kept
to himself, unless an emergency happened. Quite un-
consciously Ricky opened his mind to thoughts from
that direction, to see whether it was a good time to
visit his father's cabin.

The violence of the thought he received nearly
knocked him over. What on Lambda was stirring old
Doc J. up to such an extent? And—bother, he was
talking to somebody—Woodman, apparently. Ricky,
unlike Big Sword, could still pick up thought at the
moment when it drained into the level of speech, but
even for him it was highly indistinct. He strained,
trying to catch the cause of all this commotion. Woodman had found something—something unpleasant—
something—

Ricky dashed out of the cabin door and crossed the
half-dozen yards that separated his hut from his father's. Just outside the voices were clearly distinct;
Woodman was speaking excitedly and loudly.

"It was absolutely devilish! Oh, I suppose it was
physical—some sort of miasma—in fact it nearly knocked
me down, but it felt just exactly as though somebody
were standing and hating me a few yards off. Like
that feeling you get after space 'flu, as though nobody
loves you, only this was magnified about a million

times—the most powerful depressant ever, and absolutely in the open air, too."

"Where was this?"

"The eighth sector—just about here."

He was evidently pointing to a map. Cold with apprehension, Ricky deliberately tried to probe into his father's mind, to see just what they were looking at. The picture was fuzzy and danced about, but he could see the pointer Jordan was using—the ivory stylus he always carried, and—yes, that was the clearing in the forest that housed the Tree itself! The guards about it had been all too successful in their efforts to keep intruders away.

Jordan laughed harshly. "Do you remember that we scheduled this planet as safe?" He got to his feet. "First Barney encounters devils and now you've discovered the Upas Tree. You're sure this gas or whatever it is came from the plants?"

"I'm certain it was this one particular tree. It's by itself in the middle of an open space. The feeling began when I was six feet from it. It has big pods—they may secrete the toxic—I collected a branch once before and didn't feel anything. Perhaps it's seasonal."

"Well, it'll have to come down." Ricky, horrified, felt his father's savage satisfaction at coming across an enemy he could deal with. "Ellen wants to push her soil examinations out in that direction—it's the only sector we haven't covered yet and a good many people want to work there."

Ricky, horrified, straightened from his crouching position under the window and appeared like a jack-in-the-box over the sill.

"You mustn't, Doc! Honestly you mustn't. That Tree's terribly important. It's only—"

"Ricky!" Jordan lunged to his feet, scattering objects across his desk. "Were you listening to my conversation?"

Ricky turned white. "Yes, I was, but—"

"Go to your cabin."

Woodman made a move to intervene, but Jordan brushed it aside.

"I'll speak to you later. For the moment, you'll go to your cabin and stay there, until I have time to deal with you."

Woodman thought that Ricky was about to make some further protest, but after a moment's tension he turned and bolted.

Jordan picked up the stylus with a trembling hand.

"I'll come with you and investigate this thing at once, Woodman. We'll need masks and an air-sampler, and we may as well take one of those portable detection kits. Can you draw them from the store, please, and be ready in ten minutes. Get a blaster, too."

Woodman thought of arguments and decided against them. Old Jordan had been stewing up for something like this for the last week and it was probably better to let him get it out of his system. When it came to the point Jordan wouldn't start destroying things without careful consideration; he was too good a scientist for that. Woodman didn't know why Ricky was so concerned, but he himself would take good care that a possibly unique specimen wasn't damaged in a hurry. He went for the equipment.

Jordan hesitated at the entrance to Ricky's cabin. He heard a slight movement within, and moved on. He was still trembling with a fury that he only half understood, and knew that he was in no state to conduct a delicate interview, or even to think straight. Better leave the boy alone until he had got things sorted out in his own mind.

Ricky, lying tense on his bunk, "listened" with all his power. Old Woodman didn't really approve of this expedition, made in such a hurry. Good. Doc J. was half aware that his own brain wasn't working straight. Good again. Ricky spared a moment to wish that he had given more thought to his father during the last week, but it was too late for that now. Even if Jordan didn't take a blaster to the Tree straight off, the People were still perched on the thin edge of disaster. For the first time since he had understood what Big Sword wanted him to do, Ricky began to doubt whether it could be done. Were people going to listen to him? Were Doc J. and Woodman and Miss Ellen and the rest of them really any different from Cora and Camillo and all the other people on Earth who didn't even try to understand?

No, there was only one way to make the People

safe—if it would work. And he'd *got* to take it. Because this was his own fault for not telling Doc J. sooner. He'd acted like a silly kid, wanting to keep his secret to himself just a little longer. Well, now he was going to put things right, if he could—righter than they were before. With any luck it would be hours before anyone missed him. He might even be able to do what he wanted and call back on his transmitter to explain before they found that he had gone.

Ricky was already out of the clearing before Jordan, who had started out with Woodman, turned back to speak to Dr. Scott.

"Ellen, I've left Ricky in his cabin. We had a . . . disagreement. I think he's better left to himself just now, but would you mind going to his cabin in an hour or so, to see that he's all right?"

"Of course, John. But what—?"

"No time now. I'll explain later. Thank you, Ellen. Good-bye."

There was no undergrowth in the forest but the branches were extremely thick and the darkness beneath them almost complete. Jordan, following Woodman through the trees and the slow pace enforced by these conditions, felt his anger drain away and a deep depression take its place. What sort of showing had he made, either as a father or as the head of the expedition? This particular episode was quite idiotic. There was nothing in Woodman's report to call for this immediate dash into the forest. He should at least have stopped to find out what Ricky knew about it—and now that he was cooling off, Ricky's anxiety seemed more and more puzzling. If it weren't that to turn back would make him look even more of a fool than he did already, he would have given up and gone to find out what the boy knew.

In front of him Woodman came to a halt.

"That's it, sir! That's the Tree! But—there's no feeling about it now."

Jordan brushed past him.

"Stay here. Be ready to put your mask on." He walked slowly forward until he was right under the branches of the Tree.

On either side of the clearing, sitting in the treetops, the Guardians consulted anxiously.

"The Contact said we must not drive them away. We must do as he suggested."

Jordan looked up at the branches and dared them to depress him.

"I don't feel anything," he said at last. "Woodman, are you certain this is the right tree?"

"Well, I was, sir." Woodman approached it in growing doubt. "All these little clearings are so much alike, I could have—no, it is the right one! I tied my handkerchief to this branch for a marker, before I bolted. Here it is."

The Guardians gave the telepathic equivalent of a sigh and started on the next line of defense.

"You know, sir—" Woodman was carefully deferential—"I've never seen another specimen like this. After all, this little bit of the forest is pretty well cut off—the Rift on one side, the Mountains on the other and the River in the south. This type of soil doesn't even extend as far as the River. You might get forms here which were unique—relics, or species evolved since the Rift opened. I don't feel we ought to destroy it without very good reason."

Jordan scowled up at the nearest pod.

"I wasn't proposing to destroy it here and now! If the thing is a potential menace we must find out about it, that's all. I must say I don't . . . what's that?"

The sound of snapping twigs could be heard back along the path. Woodman started down it with Jordan at his heels; it was so dark that he was almost on top of Dr. Scott before he saw her.

"John! Thank goodness. Listen, you've got to come back at once. It's . . . it's Ricky. He's gone. I went to his cabin like you said, and he wasn't there. He isn't anywhere in camp. He's gone."

There was a flurry in the camp, but it was an organized flurry. Jordan, white and sick-looking, nevertheless had himself well under control. Important facts were sorted out quickly.

Three parties working on the east side of the clearing could swear that Ricky had not passed them.

Various delicate gadgets which responded violently to the movement of humans anywhere near them were rigged in the wood to the north, which was taboo in consequence. They showed no sign of disturbance.

That left the south and the west. South was a stretch of about eight miles of forest, unbroken until it reached the big river. West was about half a mile of forest, fairly well explored, and then the Great Rift.

"There'd be no sense in going that way," Jordan laid a pointer on the map to indicate the Rift; he noticed in a detached way that his hand was quite steady. "It doesn't lead anywhere. There's just one place he could be making for, if we assume him to have an intelligible plan, and that is the First Base on the coast. The one way he could possibly get there would be to get to the river and float down it on one of the log rafts—we saw plenty of them coming down while we were at the base."

"But the rapids—" said somebody.

"Has anyone reason to suppose that Ricky knew about the rapids?" Beads of sweat stood out on Jordan's forehead. No one answered. "We have to find him before he gets there. Unless any of you can suggest another way he might be trying to go."

Nobody cared to suggest that Ricky, if he had flung off in blind panic, might be headed nowhere in particular under the shade of the black trees. On the south side the paths went only for half a mile or so, and if he left them he could be lost within a hundred yards of the camp. They had already tried to pick up the tracker he was supposed to carry, but he had evidently switched it off or thrown it away.

The geologist, Penn, spoke suddenly from the back of the group.

"How about the Rift? It interested him. He might try to get across."

"That's possible," said Jordan. "On the Rift he'd be relatively easy to spot. That's why I propose to leave it till later. We have only one heliflier. If he's gone through the forest to the river we have to catch him at once. He's been gone two and a half hours. If he went straight to the nearest point of the river he might be there by now. The heliflier's the only chance. I can patrol the whole stretch and spot him as soon as he comes to it. If he hasn't reached it by dawn, I'll go back and fly over the Rift. If he does happen to be there, he won't take much harm in that time."

"There are two helifliers," someone suggested.

"No," said Jordan sharply. "The other is unsafe."

Not all the party were to join the hunt at once.

"There are only a few profitable lines," said Jordan. "We don't want everybody exhausted at the same time. This may be more than one day's search. And some of you have long-term observations to continue." He raised his hand, stilling a protest. "If to take all of you would increase the . . . the speed with which we are likely to find Ricky by one per cent, or half that, I'd take you all. But I won't ruin several months' work for nothing."

In the end several parties set out through the trees

south and one went west. Jordan had already taken the one serviceable heliflier and departed. They had arranged an automatic sound-signal to go off every half hour in the clearing, in case Ricky was lost and trying to find his way back, and there were flares and a searchlight for when it became dark.

Ellen Scott had been left behind as part of the "reinforcements." She managed to catch Woodman before his party left.

"You used the second heliflier, didn't you? What's wrong with it?"

Woodman grimaced. "It failed to cooperate over landing. I got down intact by the skin of my incisors and had to walk home—we fetched it finally on the truck. I found a rough patch on one of the power planes and cleaned it up. That may or may not have been the cause of the trouble. We haven't got checking equipment here and nobody's tried it out the hard way. Leave it alone, Ellen. When those things are good they're very very good. Once they act up—leave them alone. It wouldn't be any use over the forest and Doc J. won't miss anything on the River."

"How about the Rift?"

"Why should he go there? He was upset but he wasn't crazy. No, he must have set out for the base camp— probably thinks he'll be treated as a hero if he gets there. I'll give him heroics next time we meet."

Ellen was occupied for the next hour with various laboratory jobs to be done for the members of the search party. Reports came in every few minutes over the radio, but they were all negative. The ground was hard dry. If Ricky had stuck to the broken trails, he would leave no sign. Even off them, he was small enough to walk under the trees where a grown man would have had to push his way through. There were three chances: to see him from the air, to get a fix on his radio, and to come upon him among the trees. And however systematic the searchers were they knew perfectly well that they could only do that by chance.

Unless one could guess where he had gone. Jordan thought he had guessed.

Ellen prowled restlessly about. What would Ricky have done? Nothing had been taken from his room; had he set out without any equipment at all?

She went to the kitchen. Barney was muddling around among his cupboards, in a very bad mood. He had wanted to go with the search parties and had been turned down.

"Barney," said Ellen quickly, "did Ricky take any food?"

"That's what I'm trying to check, Miss. There's some biscuits gone, I think. He could have taken them, or it could have been anyone this afternoon. And I think one of the big canteens has gone, but I suppose a search party took it."

"They didn't," said Ellen sharply. "There are always plenty of streams, apart from the pools in the leaves. They only took small water bottles."

"One of the big canteens has gone," repeated Barney obstinately. "And one of the water bottles isn't, if you take my meaning—Ricky did not take one of those, I mean, I've accounted for them. The canteen I can't account for. But Ricky wouldn't lumber himself up with that," he added morosely. "He couldn't carry it if it was more than half full, and he knows about the streams as well as anybody. No, I reckon someone pinched it for a collecting tin or something. That's how it goes in this place, and now we can see what comes of it. You can't keep a proper check on anything—"

But Dr. Scott had gone.

She waited, fuming, until the party which had gone west came back.

"Yes, we looked over the Rift all right," said the leader morosely. "Hell, Ellen, the whole place is a heat-trap. With the haze and flickers visibility is about twenty yards. Even from the air you wouldn't see anything, unless maybe when the shadows get longer and before they get too long. Jordan wouldn't see anything if he did fly over it now. Besides, why should the kid have gone into that oven?"

Ellen turned away. Why should Ricky have gone that way? But why should he have taken a big canteen, unless he was going to cross a waterless area? If he had taken it, of course. But there were plenty of containers in the stores for scientific work.

Ricky had been interested in the Rift, certainly. He had been asking questions about it yesterday—one of

the few times lately he had shown interest in anything
at all.

But visibility in the Rift was bad now. When the
shadows were longer—

Jordan called over the radio. He had been flying up
and down the river and the adjacent forest for the last
hour and a half. Ricky had been gone about four hours.

There were three hours of daylight left.

Two hours later the situation was unchanged. To
the parties in the forest night would make little difference; they were using lights already. Jordan pro-
posed to stay in the air—one or other of the moons
would be in the sky most of the night. There was about
one hour of daylight left.

Ellen Scott listened to his report, and those of the
search parties. Then she went briskly to the place
where the one remaining heliflier was parked. She
found another member of the expedition contemplating
it gloomily.

"Come away from there, Phil," she said severely.

"Oh, hell, Ellen, there's a seventy-five per cent chance
the thing's all right. Woodman said he'd fixed up a
rough plane, didn't he?" The man turned away nevertheless. "What in Space did Jordan want to bring that
kid here for?"

Ten minutes later he shot out of his cabin, where
he had been dispiritedly collecting together the mak-
ings of a drink, in time to see the heliflier rise gently
into the air and disappear toward the west.

*   *   *

Although the shadows were beginning to lengthen, the Rift was like a furnace. The water in the canteen was hot. Ricky and Big Sword sat in the slightly cooler earth on the north of a boulder and contemplated the forest lying away to the left—not the forest they knew, but the strange trees of the farther side.

Big Sword's goggle eyes did not register emotion, but Ricky could feel the stir of curiosity in him. Big Sword was already reaching out to new streams, new treetops, new bare places that would be warm in the sun. For himself Ricky could only think about the two miles remaining to be walked.

He had hopelessly underestimated the time it would take him to pick his way through eight miles of boulders, too hot for the hand, walking on sliding shingle; he had managed less than two miles an hour. But now he had to get on. He stirred himself, got Big Sword perched again on his shoulder and restrapped the canteen, lighter now but still a burden.

He had gone perhaps a dozen strides when the shadow of the heliflier came up behind and settled over his head.

Ricky started to run. There was no sense to it, and Big Sword disliked the effects, but he ran just the same, with the water sloshing about his back. The shadow of the flier slid forward a hundred yards and it began to come down over a comparatively level place. Ricky swerved sideways. He heard a shout echo among

the boulders, but the echo of combined relief and ex-
asperation in his mind rang louder.

"Ricky! Stop and talk! Whatever it is, I'll help. There's
no sense in running. If I get in touch with your father
there'll be another flier and several people here in
twenty minutes. Stop! Listen to me, will you, you—"

The shouts echoed on for a moment, but the thought
had stopped.

Dr. Scott came whirling up through hot red mists
to find herself lying beside a fire. A very hot fire, in
a stone fireplace. It didn't make sense. Warm water
was being sloshed across her face and there was a
murmur of voices—two of them.

"She hit her head. That's all. She fainted. She'll
come round in a minute. Then you'll hear her. It isn't
sleep, no—not exactly. What's the matter? Why don't
you—"

The second voice was no more than a vague murmur
of curiosity; it was beginning to sound irritated as well.

Ellen remembered that she had been running among
a lot of boulders and had twisted her foot. No doubt
she had hit her head when she fell; certainly it ached.
But what had she been doing that for?

She opened her eyes.

Ricky's anxious face hung directly above her and he
was pouring water from his cupped hand on to her
forehead. Beside him was—

Ellen winced and shut her eyes.

"Dr. Scott. Please!" Ricky sounded worried. "Are you hurt?"

"Delirious, I think," said Ellen faintly. She opened her eyes again. "Where did it go?"

Ricky's face was a study in doubt and other emotions. Ellen put a hand to the aching spot on the back of her head and began very cautiously to sit up.

"Come on, Ricky," she said firmly. "Who were you talking to?"

"Aloud?" said Ricky, in tones of surprise. "Oh, so that's why he couldn't hear."

Ellen shut her eyes again. "I'm the one with concussion, not you," she pointed out. "Who couldn't hear?"

"Well, his *name's* Big Sword," said Ricky doubtfully. "More or less, that is. He says he's coming back, anyway."

Ellen opened her eyes once more. They focused on the region of Ricky's right ear. Laid gently over it was a skinny black hand with four long, many-jointed fingers. A slender arm stole into view, attached to what might have been a medium-sized potato that had happened to grow black. On top of this was perched a head about the size of a large egg. The greater part of this was occupied by two large light-gray eyes with slit pupils and dully shining surfaces. They goggled at her solemnly.

Once again she was aware of a vague murmur of curiosity, not divisible into words.

Ellen drew a deep breath. "Ricky, this . . . this friend of yours. Why did you bring him here?"

Ricky studied her face earnestly. "It was my idea, not his, Dr. Scott. I wanted to get to the forest over there. To the other side of the Rift."

"But why?"

Ricky shook his head.

"It wasn't that at all. It was my idea, I tell you, not Big Sword's. He didn't . . . didn't hypnotize me. He wouldn't have done it to Barney except that he couldn't think of anything else to do. And I've absolutely got to get there now!"

Ellen sat up and stared at him. "All right, Ricky. Listen, you tell me the reason. If it's a good one . . . well, I must let your father know you're safe. But I won't tell him where you are. I'll fly you to the forest, and then back. How about that?"

Ricky breathed a sigh of relief. "Yes," he said. "Is Doc J. very worried?"

"Worried? Listen, make it quick. I'm going to call him in ten minutes, whatever. What are you doing here?"

Ricky sighed and closed his eyes for a moment. "The idea began with the jellyfish, really," he said. "The male jellyfish in the lake."

The heliflier had completed the fifth sweep down the river to the sea; back up the river to the rapids, where many rafts of floating vegetation broke up and reformed, making Jordan's heart jump as he hovered above them; on up the river to the point he had fixed as farthest east. It was no good to fly over the forest; he had found that he could not pick up the search parties when he knew they were directly below him. The river was his only hope.

Nearly time to make another report. His hand was on the button of the radio when the speaker came suddenly to life.

"Calling all search parties. John Jordan please answer. Can you hear?"

Jordan's voice came out as a harsh croak. "I hear. Is he—"

"Ricky's safe. He's with me now. Turn everyone home. But—listen. He had a good reason for going off as he did. He had something to do and it's not finished. So I'm not going to tell you where we are."

Jordan shouted something incoherent, but her voice overrode him.

"It's important, John. I don't know if it will come off, but he must have a chance to try. You can probably find out where we are, but—don't come. Do you understand?"

"Ellen, is he really all right? And are you?"

"Sure I'm all right. We're going to remain all right. We'll be back some time next morning. Oh, and Ricky says"—her voice broke off for a moment—"Ricky says he is very sorry to have worried you, honestly he is, but it was urgent, and will you please not do anything to damage that Tree." There was a moment's silence. "John? You haven't done something to it already?"

"I haven't, no."

"Don't let anyone touch it. Good night, John. Sleep well."

"Ellen—"

The speaker clicked and was silent.

The helifliers were designed for sleeping in, in an emergency, but they were not air-conditioned. Ellen felt the compress on her head, which had long ceased to be cold, and envied bitterly Ricky's ability to sleep under these conditions. A faint gleam of light from button-sized surfaces a couple of yards off showed that Big Sword was still sitting and watching as he had been doing ever since they lay down. Ellen wished bitterly that she had had the sense to lie beside the refrigerator so that she could get more cold water without having to lift her aching head.

The gray buttons moved. She felt small, strong fingers tugging gently at the compress. She lifted the compress off her head and felt it go. There was a sound of faint movement and the click of the refrigerator door, with a momentary blast of lovely cold air. A few minutes later the compress, beautifully cold now, was poked carefully back under her head. She felt the thistledown touch of skinny fingers against her cheek.

"Thank you," she murmured, and then, remembering, she repeated it inside her head, "Thank you, Big Sword."

They had flown at dawn and the heliflier sat among the boulders at the foot of the cliff. Ellen and Ricky sat beside it, shivering a little in the morning cold, and waited.

Ellen looked at Ricky's intent face. He could not hear strange members of the People distinctly, she had gathered, but he could usually detect their presence.

"What does it feel like?" she asked abruptly.

"Hearing thoughts?" Ricky considered. "It feels like thinking. You can't really tell other thoughts from your own—unless they've been specially directed. That's what made it all so very difficult."

"I see," Ellen sighed. What on Earth, or of it, could Ricky's future be? True telepaths would not fit in Earth's scheme of things.

"I used to pick up thoughts all the time," Ricky went on. "I didn't know that until I found out how to shut them off. It was a sort of fuzzy background to my thinking. Do you know, I think all real good thinkers must be people with no telepathy, or else they learn to shut it right off. Now I can do that I think much clearer."

"So you don't overhear thoughts accidentally now?" Ellen felt encouraged.

"No, I don't. I only get directed thoughts. I'm not

going to overhear anyone ever again, it's just a nuisance."

"Stick to that. I don't think uncontrolled telepathy is much good to a human being."

"It isn't. I tell you what, I think there are two ways of evolving communication, telepathy and communication between senses, and people who are good at the one aren't good at the other. I'll never be a real good communicator like the People, my mind doesn't work the right way. But I'll be good enough to be useful for research. I'm going to—" Ricky broke off, seized his companion's arm and pointed.

Ellen looked up at the cliff. It was about thirty feet high, here, with only a couple of six-inch ledges to break the sheer drop. Black foliage overhung it in places.

"There!" whispered Ricky. Slowly there came into view a black head the size of an egg—a black head in which eyes shone gray.

"Is he coming back?" whispered Ellen. "Has he given up, then?"

There was a faint rustling among the leaves. Ricky's grip tightened painfully on her arm.

A second black head appeared beside the first.

"You see," said Ricky anxiously, "I didn't really think you'd go and destroy the Tree straight off, but I couldn't be sure. And everyone was angry with me about one thing or another and I didn't know if they'd listen."

"Speaking for myself," said Woodman, "there were one or two moments when if I'd had a blaster handy the Tree would have been done for there and then."

"So you were just taking out insurance," said Jordan.

"Yes, because if we found other Trees the species would continue anyway. Big Sword and I meant to ask you to help about that, later—the Journey, I mean—only then I thought we'd better try that straight away in case I was stopped later. I thought if I could *show* people, it was better than telling them."

"Isn't Big Sword coming?" said another of the party. The whole of the expedition, including even Barney, was seated around a square table raised on trestles in the center of the clearing. Ricky nodded.

"As soon as we're ready," he said. "Now, if you like. But he says if too many people think at him at once it may hurt, so he wants you to be ready to start talking if I give the signal."

"What about?" said Cartwright.

"Anything. Anything at all. Shall I call him?"

There was half a minute's expectant silence. Then lightly as a grasshopper Big Sword flew over Ellen's head and landed with a slight bounce in the center of the table.

There was a simultaneous forward movement of heads as everybody bent to look at him, and he sat up and goggled out of pale bulging eyes. Then—

Most of them felt the sharp protest of discomfort

before Ricky waved his hand. Nobody had really thought out what to say and there was a moment of silence, then somebody began to talk about the weather, the statistician began on the multiplication table, Jordan found himself muttering, " 'Twas brillig, and the slithy toves . . ."—after a minute or so only Ricky was still silent.

"He says he'll go to one person after another, but the rest keep talking," reported Ricky presently. "You can ask him to do things if you like."

Solemnly Big Sword went round the table, sitting for a few moments in front of each person, snapping out his membranes, revolving to present his back view, and then going on.

"That's him!" said Barney as Big Sword came to a halt in front of him. "But how did he sting me?"

The spindly hand whipped to Big Sword's flat thigh and flashed back holding a flat gray spike two and a half inches long. He held it out and Barney fingered the point in a gingerly fashion.

"That's the sword, is it?" murmured Woodman. "Do they secrete it, Ricky?"

"I think so, but I haven't asked him."

Woodman breathed out a long sigh.

"This," he said, "is the answer to a biologist's prayer."

Big Sword bounced suddenly back into the middle of the table. "He's tired," said Ricky. "He says he'll send someone else another day." Ricky yawned uncontrollably as Big Sword took a flying leap off the table and hopped across the clearing. He had had a hard day the day before and a very early start this morning and a lot of excitement since.

"Can we just have the story straight?" said the statistician suddenly. "The biological story, I mean. You people may have been able to follow it through all the interruptions, but I didn't. I gathered that Ricky had discovered the female of the species, but that's all. How did they get lost?"

"I'll tell it," said Jordan, looking at Ricky, who was nodding sleepily, "and Ricky can correct me. Big Sword's People are the active and intelligent offspring of an organism which to all intents and purposes is a large tree. They are produced by an asexual budding process inside pods. When they are a year or so old they are seized by the urge to migrate across the Rift. They never knew why, and probably none of them ever got across. It occurred to Ricky that alternation of generations usually turns out to have sex at the bottom of it. Big Sword's People couldn't reproduce themselves—they simply hatched from the Tree. So Ricky thought that there might be another Tree on the other side of the Rift which produced females. And when I very foolishly considered destroying the Tree because of Woodman's experience, he thought he had to go and find them straight off, so that at least the species would survive. And I'm glad to say he was quite right—they were there."

"You mean to say," said Cartwright, "that the Tree

has been producing People for the last fifteen thousand years without a sexual generation at all?"

"Not necessarily," said Woodman. "There may have been several on this side of the Rift, at first, and this Tree may be the last offspring of a small population. It must have been an outlier, if so, because the migration was so firmly set for the west."

"And there's another tree on the far side which produces females?"

"There are two female trees and three that bear males, but two of the male ones are very old and have few offspring, and none of the seeds have been fertile for at least fifty generations. Apparently not many come to full maturity at the best of times, but this outcross may really save the species."

"And what exactly is the plan?" demanded the statistician. "To ferry them across? What will they do when we leave?"

"No," said Jordan. "We don't propose to interfere more than we have to. The tragedy of the whole process was that the People who took the Journey almost certainly died on the way. Twelve miles in the sun, with no water, was too much for them. We propose to provide a green belt—a black belt rather—along the migration route. Tiven is looking into the possibilities—"

Tiven looked up from his slide rule. "Easy as π," he said cheerfully. "We can make the channel in a week, once we get the digger from First Base, and a cooker for concrete, and there are any number of streams which run down to the Waste and then vanish underground. It's just a question of training one of them in the way it should go, and protecting it from evaporation in the first year or two until the vegetation gets thick enough."

The conversation flowed on. But Ricky, his head resting on the table, was already asleep.

Jordan stood at the edge of the Rift and looked over the embryo river-valley that Tiven had designed. Seedlings had been planted along the channel, in earth transported for that purpose, and were already taking hold. The revolving sun-cutters designed to protect them at this stage and to stop excessive evaporation gave the whole thing a mechanical air at present, but they would be done within a year or two; they were designed to go to dust then, so that even if the expedition had to leave they would not be left. There are places for poorly built things!

Two of the People shot down the cliff a little to one side and disappeared into the shade along the channel.

"Are they off on the Journey?" said Ellen Scott.

"I don't think so. They go singly, as a rule. No, I think . . . look there!"

There were four People now at the end of the line of saplings. Two were presumably the ones who had passed a few minutes before; the other two were linked hand in hand and bore across their shoulders a kind of yoke with a long pod dangling from it. The two from the near side of the forest had taken the hands of the newcomers and were helping them up the cliff.

"This is the result of your soil report, I think," said Jordan. "Woodman says that one reason for the lack of germination on the other side is the exhaustion of the few pockets of suitable soil. I wonder whether it was the necessity of finding the right soil, as well as of looking after the seedling, that led them to develop intelligence?"

The two newcomers had reached the top of the cliff. They seemed hardly to notice the helpers, nor did the latter seem to expect it. The burdened couple moved slowly along, pausing every now and then to investigate the soil. They stopped close to Ellen's feet and prodded carefully.

"Not here, little sillies!" she murmured. "Farther in."

John smiled. "They've got plenty of time. One couple planted their pod just under one of Branding's tripods; trying not to step on them drove him nearly crazy. He had to move the whole lot in the end. It takes them weeks sometimes to find a spot that suits them."

"Continuing the species," said Ellen thoughtfully. "I always thought it sounded rather impersonal."

Jordan nodded. "The sort of thing you can take or leave," he agreed. "I used to think that you could either explore space or you could . . . well, continue the species is as good a way of putting it as any. Not both."

"I used to think that, too."

"Once it was true. Things have changed, even in the last few years. More and more people are organizing their lives to spend the greater part of them away from Earth. Soon there's going to be a new generation whose home isn't on Earth at all. Children who haven't been to Terrestrial schools, or played in Terrestrial playrooms, or watched the Terrestrial stereos, or—"

"Suffered the benefits of an advanced civilization?"

"Exactly. How do you feel about it, Ellen? Or . . . that's a shirker's question. Ellen Scott, will you marry me?"

"So as to propagate the species?"

"Blast the species! Will you marry me?"

"What about Ricky?"

"Ricky," said Jordan, "has been careful to let me know that he thinks it would be a very suitable match."

"The devil he has! I thought—"

"No telepathy involved. If everyone else knows I love you, why shouldn't he? Ellen—did I say please, before? Ellen, please, will you marry me?"

There was a silence. Depression settled on Jordan. He had no right to feel so sure of himself. Ellen was ten years younger and had a career to think of. He had made a mess of one marriage already and had a half-grown son. He had taken friendliness for something else and jumped in with both feet much too soon. He had made a fool of himself—probably.

"Well?" he said at last.

Ellen looked up and grinned.

"I was just making sure. I'm not quite certain I could take being married to a telepath—which you are not, my dear. Absolutely not. Of course I'm going to."

Ricky, with Big Sword on his shoulder, was strolling along a path in the sun. He saw his father and Dr. Scott return to the camp arm in arm, and nodded with satisfaction. About time, too. Now perhaps Doc J. would stop mooning around and get on with his work for a change. He'd had Ricky and Woodman's last report on the biology of the People for two weeks without making the slightest attempt to read it, and it was full of interesting things.

Just for a moment, Ricky wondered what it was like to get all wrapped up in one individual like that. No doubt he'd find out in time. It would have to be somebody interested in real things, of course—not an Earthbound person like poor Cora.

Meanwhile he was just fourteen and free of the Universe, and he was going to have fun.

Big Sword, from his perch on Ricky's shoulder, noticed the couple with the pod. He saw that this one was fertile, all right—the shoot was beginning to form inside it. One of them was an old friend from this side of the Rift, but it was no good trying to talk to him—his mind would be shut. The whole process of taking the Journey, finding a mate and taking care of one's seedling was still a mystery to Big Sword in the sense that he could not imagine what it felt like. Just now he was not very interested. He had nearly a year in which to find out things, especially things about the Big People who, now they were domesticated, had turned out to be so useful, and he was going to enjoy that and not speculate about the Journey, and what it felt like to take it.

Because, eventually, the call would come to him, too, and he would set off up the new little stream to the other side of the Rift where the trees of the Strangers grew. And then he would know.

The Gift

by Ray Bradbury

Here is a story that answers the question "What will be tomorrow's Statue of Liberty for immigrants into space?"

It would be Christmas tomorrow, and even while the three of them rode to the rocket port the mother and father were worried. It was the boy's first flight into space, his very first time in a rocket, and they wanted everything to be perfect. So when, at the custom's table, they were forced to leave behind his gift, which exceeded the weight limit by no more than a few ounces, and the little tree with the lovely white candles, they felt themselves deprived of the season and their love.

The boy was waiting for them in the Terminal room. Walking toward him, after their unsuccessful clash with the Interplanetary officials, the mother and father whispered to each other.

"What shall we do?"

"Nothing, nothing. What *can* we do?"

"Silly rules!"

"And he so wanted the tree!"

The siren gave a great howl and people pressed forward into the Mars Rocket. The mother and father walked at the very last, their small pale son between them, silent.

"I'll think of something," said the father.

"What . . . ?" asked the boy.

And the rocket took off and they were flung headlong into dark space.

The rocket moved and left fire behind and left Earth behind on which the date was December 24, 2052, heading out into a place where there was no time at all, no month, no year, no hour. They slept away the rest of the first "day." Near mid-night, by their Earth-time New York watches, the boy awoke and said, "I want to go look out the porthole."

There was only one port, a "window" of immensely thick glass of some size, up on the next deck.

"Not quite yet," said the father. "I'll take you up later."

"I want to see where we are and where we're going."

"I want you to wait for a reason," said the father.

He had been lying awake, turning this way and that, thinking of the abandoned gift, the problem of the season, the lost tree and the white candles. And at last, sitting up, no more than five minutes ago, he believed he had found a plan. He need only carry it out and this journey would be fine and joyous indeed.

"Son," he said, "in exactly one-half hour it will be Christmas."

"Oh," said the mother, dismayed that he had mentioned it. Somehow she had rather hoped that the boy would forget.

The boy's face grew feverish and his lips trembled. "I know, I know. Will I get a present, will I? Will I have a tree? You promised—"

"Yes, yes, all that, and more," said the father.

The mother started. "But—"

"I mean it," said the father. "I really mean it. All that and more, much more. Excuse me, now I'll be back."

He left them for about twenty minutes. When he came back he was smiling. "Almost time."

"Can I hold your watch?" asked the boy, and the watch was handed over and he held it ticking in his fingers as the rest of the hour drifted by in fire and silence and unfelt motion.

"It's Christmas *now*! Christmas! Where's my present?"

"Here we go," said the father and took his boy by the shoulder and led him from the room, down the hall, up a rampway, his wife following.

"I don't understand," she kept saying.

"You will. Here we are," said the father.

They had stopped at the closed door of a large cabin. The father tapped three times and then twice in a code.

The door opened and the light in the cabin went out and there was a whisper of voices.

"Go on in, son," said the father.

"It's dark in there."

"I'll hold your hand."

They stepped into the room and the door shut, and the room was very dark indeed. And before them loomed a great glass eye, the porthole, a window four feet high and six feet wide, from which they could look out into space.

The boy gasped.

Behind him, the father and mother gasped with him, and then in the dark room some people began to sing.

"Merry Christmas, son," said the father.

And the voices in the room sang the old, familiar carols, and the boy moved forward slowly until his face was pressed against the cool glass of the port. And he stood just looking and looking out into space and the deep night at the burning and the burning of ten billion white and lovely candles. . . .